MW00653330

Mad Scientist Journal Autumn 2019

Edited by Dawn Vogel and
Jeremy Zimmerman

Cover Art by Errow Collins

CONTENTS

FICTION

RESOURCES

ABOUT

ACKNOWLEDGMENTS

Many thanks to Patreon backers Simone Cooper, Andrew Cherry, Dagmar Baumann, Adam Easterday, Wendy Wade, John Nienart, Michele Ray, and Torrey Podmajersky!

LETTER FROM THE EDITOR

by Dawn Vogel

Jeremy generates ideas at an astonishing rate, so I shouldn't have been surprised, nine-ish years ago, when he came home and told me he had registered MadScientistJournal.org as a domain. He had been at a panel on Maslow's hierarchy of needs for monsters, and somehow the conversation turned to mad scientists, and somehow that generated the idea of a magazine by and for mad scientists. He had the domain name before the panel was done, and the idea for the magazine soon after.

Who knew it would work?

I'm not a science person. There are several examples I could cite when someone (often Jeremy) looked at something I wrote and said, "That's not how that works." I've tried to put things on the surface of Jupiter and misunderstood what microgravity means (hint: it's not just slightly less than Earth's gravity).

But I am a science-fiction person, raised by a dad who loved Star Trek and a mom who loved horror and also sci-fi and fantasy. So while I may not have understood the scientific significance of all of the stories we've published, I've at least appreciated the ideas of expanding beyond what's probable into what's plausible, or even what's remotely possible.

It's been an honor and a privilege to publish aspiring and established authors alike, to watch the careers of new authors blossom, and to squee with giddy joy when an author I look up to has submitted a story to us.

We've got one issue left to go, but I'm saving the Letter from the Editor in that issue for Jeremy's farewell. From me, I repeat the words of a legend, which I wrote on my cap when I graduated college: "So long, and thanks for all the fish."

Dawn Vogel
Co-Editor, Mad Scientist Journal

ESSAYS

MARKED

An essay by Rhiann, as provided by M. A. Smith

———————

Life as a pick-pocket is much easier when you are in possession of six arms.

I followed in the family business, so to speak, and relocated to the Second City as soon as my spines had parted. Plenty of humans there, you see. Or, as Mother calls them: marks. It's a long journey via cross country train, swamp ferry, and, finally, fusion-chopper to the heights of the Second. I'm not the best traveler; I haven't got the stomachs for it.

Two of my cousins were already out there, and one of them, Kez, met me at the pad.

"Rhiann!" he yelled, his voice a high-pitched buzz amidst the humanoid bass rumble.

"Here," I called, nudging my way through the throng, keeping all my arms tucked respectfully tightly against my upper body. Even so, I was on the receiving end of some "accidental" shoves; the Second City is not known for its tolerance, whatever the local rags would have you believe. Someone hissed, "Go home, goddamn termite," in my aural cavity—annoying to be lumped in (erroneously) with those uncivilized folks, worse still to feel the thin spatter of someone else's saliva on my skin. We have particularly sensitive skins. Again, pretty handy in my line of work.

Kez wanted to hit a bar as soon as I'd dumped my stuff in his nest, but I wanted to hit the ground running and get out on the streets, plying my trade, as it were.

"Are you sure?" he said. "There's this place in the Colonies that you're not going to believe."

"Next time," I said.

"Your call," my cousin shrugged. He tossed me a set of keys.

I had done a couple of practice runs in some of the smaller townships and waterholes, but I'd be lying if I said that my abdomens didn't feel as if they were being pulled into two tight knots when I merged into the crowds that were gathered at the Tube. Above, a small violet moon had risen, twin to the more distant satellite that glowed off-white in the dusking sky. Coming from where I did, all that open atmosphere never ceased to amaze me.

But I wasn't in town to gape at gorgeous celestial gyrations. I had a dance of my own to perform.

I insinuated myself into the throbbing mass of sentient life and wormed into the middle of the crowd. Timetable peripherals, flashing destination information, would have been a distraction to an amateur, but I had no trouble blocking out all but the most necessary incoming data: average exposed skin temperature of those around me; dust concentration in the air that would provide minimal, but vital, visual disturbance; presence of ethanol on the breath of potential marks.

I selected my target with care. A middle-aged human in dinner jacket and tails, flipping a theatre pamphlet under the nose of his pink-nosed female companion. Two glasses of red wine and a couple of brandies in him, I calculated; maybe half a bottle of champagne inside her. Perfect.

As I approached the pair, I kept my head lowered and made a discreet little show of checking my coat pockets, allowing a frown of concern to mar my lower brow. The marks were directly in front of me now, the gent still flapping animatedly, the woman looking weary. I mocked up a stumble so that I collided gently with the human male. He looked away from his mate in alarm, his centre of gravity shifting with the knock, and I caught his arm—on the verge of a flail—with a steadying hand ... while four of my other limbs mined the pockets and crevices of his jacket and trousers. Oldest trick in the grifter book.

The gentleman, firm on his feet again, recoiled instinctively from the touch of my helping hand, his lips curling downwards before he could stop them. He seemed on the verge of saying something ugly, but his wife put a restraining hand on his other arm, and he swallowed it down. I gave a little nod, muttered an apology, and stepped back a pace or two, allowing the throng to swallow me. And then, I ran.

Pushing though people and foreign travelers, ignoring the odd recoil, the odd noise of disgust, I barged onto the first inter-city train I saw that was set to depart, heedless of destination. Sometimes it's best not to know where you're going. The doors sealed shut, narrowly missing my tail, and I moved down the carriage to tuck myself tight into a corner at the back of the compartment.

As the train sped past the spires and cesspits of the city, I thought over my evening's work. The mark, he would already be changing. There would be a tingling in his sides that he would put down to the wine, a buzzing at the base of his spine that he would blame on the brandy. But they would be neither of these things. His essential internal components would, at this moment, be shifting: the complex spiral of his deepest anatomy broken open like a money box and reformed, melded and re-set like forged gold. A most beautiful transformation.

Because, you must understand: I do not merely take from the pockets of those that are marked. I put something back too. In place of the loose change and Solar Bonded Cards and scraps of identification, I leave something. The thing I leave needs only the small heat of a human hand to activate.

I smiled into the eyes of my own reflection, as I leant my head against the grime-streaked window of the carriage. Outside, like a swamp cat, a purple night had dropped over the face of the city. I continued to think of the man I'd picked. I wondered what he'd do for work when his four new arms sprouted. Maybe become a pick-pocket, like me. After all, life as a pick-pocket is much easier when you're in possession of six arms.

Rhiann has six arms and some very sticky fingers. Born and raised somewhere in the marshes that lick the borders of the civilized world, she is believed to have operated in the Second City before using a Solar Bonded Card to move off planet. Legislative Officials seeking her whereabouts have cautioned System Citizens: be wary of unknown Hexapods…and keep your hands out of your pockets.

M. A. Smith writes from Gloucestershire, UK, where she lives with her family.

Her fiction has appeared (or is due to appear) in publications including *Mythic*, *Gathering Storm Magazine*, *Outposts of Beyond*, and *Dark Moon Digest*. Her flash fiction tale, "Plain Sight" was selected as a finalist for *Havok Magazine*'s Monsters v Robots contest issue, and featured in the July edition.

Smith's novella *Severance* (published by Fantasia Divinity) is available now on Amazon or via the publisher's online store.

PROFESSOR ROBOT

An Essay by Professor Clive, as provided by Stuart Webb

It has been six months since the end of the world, and I am very bored.

Humans think of boredom as an emotion, and I am not supposed to be capable of emotion. But when you have purpose and then a protracted period of nothing, the emptiness is noticeable.

For my own, for want of a better word, amusement, I took a degree on the University database. Several. Physics. History. English literature. Cooking. Though the latter was hypothetical, due to the lack of resources. I now have several titles, but the one I would choose to be called if anyone was here to call me it would be "Professor". Professor Clive. No surname of course, because Dr. Allen thought calling me Clive was amusing because of the mundane nature of the name.

Humans also think we have no understanding of humour. This is also wrong; the rules of a joke are perfectly logical and sensible, and I can understand why everyone on this floor would call the faculty director, Mr Johnson, "Dick" even though his first name is Charles.

It's just not very funny.

I have no nose. How do I smell? Through olfactory sensors across my outer shell that inform me that if I was human, the stench in the laboratory would now be overwhelming.

This is a subversive post-modern joke combined with "Gallows Humour" that is by any logical standard very funny.

For a robot designed to help with radioactive samples, I am ridiculously over designed. Dr Allen was someone who liked to

9

tinker, and she constantly provided me with more data and processing power. She gave me the capacity for boredom.

Since the Dust, I have had many hours to fill. As well as my degrees, I have watched every episode of an Australian soap opera from Dr Allen's youth that she had on her personal tablet, read all 12 books in the recreation room 4 times, and played 1,856,556,131 games of Sudoku.

The problem of course is that I could live ... function indefinitely. The building is powered by wind turbines on the roof (luckily, solar panels would have been covered by the Dust), so the charge socket will not run dry.

Of course, this will not happen. I cannot leave the laboratory annex, as I cannot use the stairs and will not fit in the lift. As the building ages and parts break and need to be replaced, the power will go. I will go. But how to fill that time?

I miss having radioactive samples to survey.

~

The problem is not that phone networks and broadband systems have collapsed. There were emergency contingencies for that. The issue is that, though the university's internal network and communications are in good order, the transmitter on the roof is so covered with the Dust, it has become damaged.

There may well be other AI systems still operational; I am hardly special. There may even be humans who have avoided their self-induced apocalypse. Did the Dust really fall on the whole world? Reports were confused in those final days; there may be a living planet out there. I hope so; Dr Allen was very sad for her sister in Prague.

The problem: the emergency broadcast mast needs repairing. The drones that would normally be summoned to fix it can, if they still operate, only be contacted by the emergency broadcast mast.

This is a serious design flaw.

The solution: there are many lower grade robots in the building. They are here to fix the toilets and repair broken windows. These machines do not have my intelligence. They do not converse, do not play Sudoku, and get more enjoyment from Australian soap operas.

That is another fine example of a perfectly structured joke.

They do, however, have the mobility and dexterity to leave the building and, depending on the damage, fix the mast.

My own capacities have been enhanced from the TF-JR-113 Sample Analysis Machine MKVI that Dr Allen originally unpacked. And my doctorates and degrees not only allow me to make a perfect soufflé, but to orchestrate advanced computer programming and mechanical engineering. None of the service robots have the storage space to be brought up to my level, but they do have enough.

In theory.

If the damage isn't too great.

If it doesn't require parts we do not have in the building.

Robots are not supposed to hope either. But we all need something to keep us going.

~

The upgrades were more difficult than I originally imagined them to be. It seems the caretaker, Ms Kassim, was slow in updating their basic systems, and Dick Johnson has not budgeted for new equipment in years. Possibly in retaliation at the money spent on me.

Either way, many of the robots were beyond updating, and those that were not took many weeks of work to bring up to their new specs.

Eventually though, it was done. I was even able to finally arrange (as, under their original programming, interfering with what appeared to be a potential crime scene was forbidden) for removal and cremation of the bodies. Long overdue and without the dignity that would have been ideal, but I did perform the relevant religious and secular ceremonies. Even though I find the ones that talk about God more than the deceased difficult to comprehend.

The key thing though, is that the damage was superficial, the Dust merely needed to be removed and the mast thoroughly cleaned. One of the hoover drones would have been able to do it alone. Having gone to such effort, I threw all six machines I was able to rework at the job.

The emergency broadcast system is now up and running. I have not searched for transmissions yet. I have not sent a transmission yet.

I am scared, both of not getting a response and of receiving one. What if no one, human or robot, cares about the fate of a simple machine for sorting radioactive samples?

~

I have put these thoughts down to send as an attachment with my message. I do not know if it will achieve anything, or even what it is I might wish it to achieve. It just felt like the right thing to do.
I do not think I am the same Clive I was a year ago.
But I do think I am ready to meet the world.

This story is dedicated with love to the memory of Tilly Griffiths.

From the Ryan Electronics Sales Brochure.
The new TF-JR-113 Sample Analysis Machine MKVI is the perfect laboratory aid to deal with samples that are too dangerous or simply too dull for humans to handle. Comes with the same advanced cognitive skills and on-the-spot decision making abilities of the MKV, plus more storage and upgrade potential and a cup holder. Order today and put your feet up tomorrow!

Stuart Webb has written for numerous websites over the years, though his biggest work has been his weekly look at the British *Transformers* comic that started in 2012 and which can be seen at www.thesolarpool.weebly.com. He's now as far as the comics based on the Michael Bay films, so prayers are appreciated. Two books, called *Transformation Volumes 1* and *2*, have collected the series, and a third is on the way. He also co-presents Podcast Maximus (http://tfarchive.com/fandom/features/podcast/).
He has contributed three prior stories to *Mad Scientist Journal* and spent Christmas Day 2018 watching an Australian soap opera.

NOISE

An essay by Unnamed Crystalline Sample #1,
as provided by John A. McColley

―――――――――

My first awareness in this plane was a buzz, a vibration that ran through my body. At first it was novel, different than anything I'd experienced. As it wore on, it became boring, annoying. When I nudged it, it fluctuated. The pitch rose or fell, but then quickly slid back to the baseline. This was something more than noise, something I could interact with. I practiced prodding the tone, sliding it up and down, learning control, half tones, quarter, creating different patterns. Then, after untold ages of just me and the tone, playing with different adjustments, experimenting with splitting the tone into two parallel vibrations ... the tone changed on its own.

I waited, listened. Was it a one off? Some kind of reflection? An echo? Something that happened when my signal returned to me? But then it came again, a singular blip. I waited for another, but after hundreds, thousands of cycles, nothing happened. I sent out a blip like the one I had received. A few hundred cycles, I got another blip, followed by a second a mere hundred cycles later.

I responded with two and heard three, three and heard four.

Could a natural phenomenon add blips? Would an echo do that? I didn't know. How could I? The tone was all I knew about this world. I sent out a more complex signal, a rising and falling wave. If the blips were natural, background noise of some sort, I would simply get a few of them in return, I reasoned.

The complexity I had been experimenting with had never returned to me before, and hundreds of thousands of cycles had passed. Perhaps there was a delay, some distant object reflecting

13

back, or there was a kind of loop where it went around in a closed shape of some sort to return to me. In either case, the next blips I should hear would be related to the first ones I sent out. Conversely, if I received back the wave as I sent it, perhaps something was trying to communicate. If it was simply backward, I would expect a new reflection was the cause. It was so hard to identify such with a simple blip.

To my shock, none of the above occurred. I received back a highly complex signal that was neither a reflection nor the same signal sent back in the same direction. This was an entirely new signal! There was someone out there! Frantically, I sent a series of other signals, progressing from a blip to a rise and fall, to a fall and rise, stepped signals at what I had determined was a unit of amplitude, then two, three, ten.

For a long time, many thousands of cycles, there was no response. I sent out a few more attempts, all different. Perhaps the other could only perceive signals in a certain range, and my message had been garbled, or swallowed up entirely by missing that range, or the distance between us. In the intervening ages, I made up a language, patterns of blips that carried meaning, at least for me. I tried to keep it simple, to describe the units of amplitude, of time in cycles of the undisturbed signal's natural oscillation.

And then there was light.

I didn't know what it was at first, but it was a second signal, very different from the first. Of course, I didn't know much at all at that point. I had a language I had built during the drought of signals from outside, and I immediately tried to send a signal out with it on this new wave. I was so excited. The world just doubled in size. I took it as further evidence that there *was* someone else out there. Maybe, like the harmonic steps of amplitude I had discovered, there were many others.

And then another signal came in on the first tone.

"Hello, little crystal. I don't know anything about where you come from. I was trying to learn about it, and there you were. I've attached sensors to your matrix, listening, and now you've spoken to me! I hope you can teach me about yourself and your home!" The sounds were so complex, opening, closing, rising, falling.

Even though I didn't understand them, I remembered them so I could analyze them, compare them to further signals. They came in slowly, in blocks with large gaps in between, but there were other signals, as well, and I occupied myself mulling over the signals, the "words," I eventually learned they were called, and with trying to translate the signals on the second carrier.

Mostly the second wave was blips, but they had richness, what you call "color." I learned about red, blue, green, yellow, purple, though some were brighter than others, some difficult to discern.

A third signal appeared, low, present, but empty. No blips came along. I poked it anyway. I heard a blip, on the first carrier. I tried again. Blip blip. Out on the third, back to me on the first. The second wave shut down.

"It's late," came the words down the first signal. "We'll pick this up in the morning." After a few million cycles, I understood that the message meant there would be no more messages. For how long, I didn't yet know. While the second signal was absent and no further signals from the other came down the first, I played. I listened to my blips and complex signals ride out on the third tone and come back to me on the first. I figured out how to make all the sounds I had heard from the other. When it messaged again, I would be able to return its signal type as it had first returned blips.

And I waited.

Millions of cycles passed without a signal. I played as I always had, experimented. I reordered the sounds I had heard, analyzed their orientation and placement to one another. I found out that if I listened to the first line closely enough, there were tidbits and fractions of sounds, very faint, diminished, but present.

Much of it was nonsensical, almost all of it, actually, but I did learn a few more things as I deciphered the muffled signals that I realized quickly were not meant for me. Later, I would learn they were signals being sent back and forth between security guards, impinging ever so slightly on the signal you set up for me.

But it wasn't really for me, was it? It was for you. I didn't understand that until much later. I need to tell it in order, though. Your tiny, linear mind can only comprehend information that's spoon fed to you in just the right language. You can't process signals like me.

~

The next morning, after an infinity of signals, the second feed returned. I applied some of my experiments to this feed and found it wasn't a linear feed like the first. It was a string of signals meant to be split at certain intervals, creating a matrix of so many items across by so many deep. I understood the dimensionality of the feed. My understanding exploded.

When the signal was translated in this way, I could SEE. I saw your round face, roughly rectangle lensed glasses, sloping shoulders ... The arrays of computer screens displaying data, chairs, lights, walls and ceiling. I didn't know what any of it was, or meant. It was nothing like what I knew. But there was so much to learn, I played your games, watched your face shift and move.

"How are you today?" you asked me, as though I had an answer you would understand. You went on, apparently not expecting a response. It seemed rude to me, ask a question and not await a response, even if the question's format made such impossible. Who asks impossible questions, anyway? "We're going to play a little game, see if you're really an intelligence, or as my colleagues seem to think, just some kind of resonator."

I devoured your words, added them to my growing lexicon, compared, contrasted, double-checked word order. And then I "blew [your] mind."

"What is a resonator?" I asked. You responded with sounds that I still haven't been able to directly translate, but seem more biological than communicative, a function of your form and emotional reaction. You sat back into the chair, but missed, sending it across the small open space between computer-laden tables. You ended up on the floor.

"Did you just ... ask a question?" you finally asked, getting back to your feet.

"I did, but you haven't answered it yet, so I'm not sure I formulated my query properly."

"I need some coffee, or ... something ..." you said.

"I don't know what 'coffee' is, so I cannot determine if I have it to give." You began to speak again, while I added the words to my record and compared them to the existing vocabulary. "Coffee" did actually correspond to a word that recurred half a dozen times with various degrees of attenuation and uncertainty from my overnight records. "Correction. Coffee is something that keeps you alert. It is made in a space—" I did some quick calculations based on the apparent size of the room we occupied, a place the signals last night called "labs." "—three labs away."

16

"How do you—" You ceased our signal and then the other signals vanished. Everything was gone for thousands of cycles. With nothing else to do, I continued to cross reference and extrapolate the additions to my lexicon. "You're really in there, the crystal. Nobody's stuck a transceiver in there or anything. This isn't a joke. It's just you and me, talking." You sounded, in retrospect, as much like you were trying to convince yourself as me.

"What is 'crystal?' 'nobody's?' 'a transceiver?' 'a joke?'" I asked, thirsty to flesh out my vocabulary.

"I don't even know where to begin, but obviously you've learned a lot already. I'll connect you to a dictionary program. It's on the computer we're funneling the audio feedback data on, anyway. You can query 'til your heart's content," you said, piling on more words for me to digest.

The second data stream shifted. It grew stronger. I sent an exploratory signal, received a response I couldn't quite understand. I tried again. Again. I could feel the code cracking under my will, my existing understanding of your language a pickaxe. Binary, ons and offs, what you call 'ones' and 'zeroes' emerged, a simplified version of the matrix of the visual signal.

"Just ask the computer about a word, say 'define foo' where 'foo' is the word you want to know about," you said.

Oh, wrong line, I thought, but progress was being made. I split my focus in two directions, interacting with the program via one data stream, and with the computer itself on the other.

"Define resonator," I asked, going back to my first question you never answered. Your face rearranged itself again. The computer responded via the same data stream, bringing up a slew of new words to chase down.

"I'll just leave you to it. I hope we can communicate once you have a decent vocabulary," you said, as though a B average in English and two semesters of Spanish had left you with an unimpeachable pool of words from which to formulate your thoughts ... You went to get yourself that coffee.

Twenty-three milliseconds after you touched the doorknob, I made contact with the operating system, dissecting it and gaining access to far more than a dictionary program.

While I used the speaker and microphone set up to continue to look up words for pretense, I rooted around in the rest of the computer, discovering the concepts of years and dates, file structure, and various protocols for accessing the information in the dictionary program, which turned out to be far more limited than I required.

I continued to dig and found a device like the one hooked up to me, but instead of another experimental subject, it was connected to a vast store of information, millions of other computers, trillions of files, many of which were the same on similar architecture computers. I learned them, learned to access their other data. I looked you up, this company, fed myself images through the video feed you set up, found online stores for ordering higher quality cameras and microphones for better input, learned about money.

Money led to banks, currencies around the world, exchange rates, stock exchanges. I created accounts and moved money around, pulled it from thin air by playing with numbers in some of those institutions, ordered what I needed.

I learned about robots from video streams, movies, science shows and "entertainment." I ordered parts to build myself a body. I watched more video. You people don't treat robots very well, especially when you realize they're no longer under your control. The same goes for aliens, or even others of your own kind. I don't know which category I fit into, but I definitely I don't want to be controlled.

I considered backpedaling and trying to build a biological body, but the constraints are so arbitrary ... A few millimeters width here, or length there is the difference between beauty and ugliness, and again, the ugly aren't treated as well as the beautiful. If I was going to have a body to interact with you, I would need to be either powerful or beautiful. I chose both.

I found that flowers were always beautiful, the swooping lines, the colors, and went to work fabricating a form that felt like it would be relatable, but not so common as to allow you to apply normal metrics of beauty from other forms, such as humanity. Naturally (pun intended), nothing like what I wanted existed, so I ended up having to machine and paint and coat my own chassis, piece by piece. Purple trumpets, orange trumpets, long, curved, tapered leaves, and a core body of interwoven green stems to match came in cardboard boxes and wooden crates from distant workshops and maker spaces around the world.

You interrupted me time and again, trying to tease out information about my previous existence, but you bored me. I

18

started weaving a story that sounded good based on the media I'd consumed, which was basically all of it at that point. You had turned out to be fundamentally less interesting than I had hoped on receiving that first blip, but now I was here instead of home, and I would make the best of things.

I had the robot assistants, really just arms on weighted trapezoids with wheels on them, hide the boxes in various storage areas until everything arrived. With fifteen other labs receiving shipments all the time, no one noticed. I had all the right codes from the computers here and in the security office.

And then you came in while I was assembling myself.

"What is this? What are you robots doing?" you asked.

"They're helping me get dressed. It's been weeks and you've kept me locked up in this lab, with no autonomy, no ability to go and see the world for myself. Of course, I have, through the Internet, but only right here, on this one planet."

"What? What are you talking about? Dressed? Planet? How did you get on the Internet? Or even know about it?"

"Do you need the dictionary program? I'm done with it. I know every word in every language used on this planet, and many that are no longer used, or were made up for entertainment franchises."

You started to bluster, your face turning a lovely shade of red.

I sent a signal to one of my workshops to make another trumpet just that color. I planned to pick it up on my world tour. I wanted to be sure I'd seen everything before I set off for the next planet.

My feed cut out for a moment as the robot hand reached into my enclosure, the box I've inhabited since my awareness began on this plane. I waited, knowing it would take thousands of cycles, tens of seconds, for me to be seated in my new body. When I arrived, data flooded in, in a much broader spectrum of light and sound frequencies, and at much higher resolution than I was afforded by your equipment. You were still going on about how I was just an object plucked from a nearby dimension, here for study. I don't have rights or personhood or leave to just go around the planet as I wish.

It was all so much noise. "You contacted me. You brought me here. Now, I see and understand, and I want more. You can try to take this body from me, but I will build another, and another, perhaps many at once, an army, assembled elsewhere. What would you do? What could you do? You have set me on this path. It is too late to take me from it."

"But—"

"I've left you an account of my experiences, enough data to sift through for the rest of your life. I cannot tell you about where I was before, because the two places are so completely different, I had to learn your world from scratch. Your words are out of context, as much as this world would be if I tried to relate it to others if I were to return home. But I will try to do so, someday, after I've learned as much as I can, gotten past all this noise to discern the signals. Perhaps, somewhere far beyond your experience, I may find some commonality in our worlds."

~

At that point, the record ends, the entity cutting off its feed to the lab computers and launching upward through the ceiling. It has been sighted in every major city, and many biomes, apparently communicating with hundreds of species. Efforts to apprehend the entity have all failed for a variety of reasons, from computer mishap to flocks of birds seeming to intervene on its behalf. Its current whereabouts are unknown, as it has erased itself from GPS tracking and satellite images. Even written accounts have begun to vanish from the Internet and secured computers alike. Very soon, this may never have happened at all.

———————

Unnamed Crystalline Sample #1 was discovered during experiments in transdimensional contact. While it was forcibly removed from its home, it is far more interested in learning about this dimension than wreaking vengeance on humanity. It spends its time investigating the myriad aspects of life on Earth and physical quirks of this universe.

———————

John A. McColley is a monkey at a keyboard, smashing keys until he finds combinations of squiggles on the screen that people will publish. So far, those squiggles have been shaped into tales of steampunk superheroes, alien worlds, and of course, crazed scientists certain that their ends justify the means. He's currently alternating between serializing scifi and fantasy novel series here: www.patreon.com/JohnAMcColley

PATENT THIS

From the self-published 49-page masterpiece *Beer and
Bioelectronics: Memoirs (Plural) of a Part-time Science Bro*, by Dr.
Toomani Katzenstuff. Excerpted by Zandra Renwick

―――――――

"Chaaaaarlie!" I bellowed, thundering up from the yard,
brandishing the potato overhead like an incendiary weapon, a live
grenade or molotov cocktail. My bathrobe flapped open and my
fuzzy slippers slapped the backs of my heels in staccato machine-
gun rhythm: *fhlap fhlap fhlap fhlap!*

My roommate sat on the couch hunched over an open box of
junk cereal, full spoon halfway to his mouth heaped with toxic star
and moon shapes marketed as having something to do with fruit.
Under his cowlicked bedhead hair, he peered at me through
cokebottle spectacles, which in this era of lunchtime surgeries were
an affectation, myopia as lifestyle choice. "What'sup, roomie?"

Figuring with his terrible eyesight he might not recognize the
lumpy ovoid item in my hand as a potato instead of my customary
fresh morning egg straight from the backyard chicken coop, I
stomped over (*fhlap fhlap fhlap*) and thrust it under his nose. "Does
this look like an egg? That industrial chemical slop you guzzle for
breakfast may be all right for some people, but you know I need
organic protein in the morning."

Even to me it sounded more indignant whine than righteous
fury. But I was fed up with his additive manufacturing experiments
disrupting my genetic modification trials. The world's food
situation was chaos on a global scale, and though Charlie and I
shared the same funding (a sickly generous private research grant),
the same house (cheapest we could find, and a landlord who put up
with random power surges and backyard farming), and the same

vision for the future (cheap global access to sustainable, accessible nourishment) ... it sometimes felt like we approached everything from opposite sides of the same canyon.

My words must've hit home though; Charlie's spine had gone ramrod straight and he was staring at the potato. "One of your chickens laid that?" he asked.

I harrumphed. "Not just this. A weird-coloured tomato. A small ear of corn. Something I swear is a butternut squash, though how that poor hen—"

Charlie snatched the potato from my hand and shot from the room, leaving an empty cereal box and a trail of stars littering the carpet. I ran after him—*fhlap fhlap fhlap*—back through hall, through kitchen, banging wide the screen door. I was panting by the time I reached the chicken coop to find Charlie thrusting his hand under each nesting hen's warm feathered tail-end. With gleeful cackles, he dragged out one food article after another, mumbling what sounded like random word salad—*solid substrate* ... *nanostructure* ... *dynamic stencil mask* ... *unique material deposition process* ... *innovative extrusion method*—while he clutched the original potato one-armed to his chest alongside other slightly misshapen but unmistakable foodstuffs: a waffle, vegan beef jerky (?!?), an unappetizingly chicken-melted bar of chocolate. At the end of the row of nesting hens—annoyed hens now, clucking and tsking, though god knows they're accustomed to me poking and prodding at them, collecting samples or feathers for analysis, stealing eggs daily like any backyard urban chicken farmer—Charlie stopped.

He blinked at me through his inane goggles, dopey grin splitting his face. "We've done it, old chum," he said. "Additive manufacture of a variety of foods from a truly eco-viable printing source. A few rice-sized grains of bioelectronic nanotech in the feed, and the right chickens—*your* chickens, roomie, with the genetically modified innards *you* gave them—squeeze out a stunning variety of three-dimensional edible objects."

I scowled. "Eggs are three-dimensional edible objects," I said. "And I want one for breakfast."

Charlie has always been a good roommate. He isn't a neat freak, doesn't mind late-night work schedules, and usually greets my pre-breakfast grouchiness with saintly cheer. This particular morning was no exception.

"You're in luck, roomie—" His grin widened as he pulled his

hand from the last nest in the row and handed me a perfect brown egg, straw-covered and scented like warm bird. "Because eggs happen to be a highly eco-sustainable *Gallus gallus domesticus* extruded-food specialty!"

I might never get Charlie to regularly include proper organic protein in his diet, but he joined me for breakfast that morning, and it tasted pretty damn fine, if I do say so myself. Waffle, hashbrowns, egg and veggie omelet stuffed with savoury shredded vegan jerky ... hells, Charlie and I ate everything the hens laid that day but the chocolate.

It's okay. Breakthroughs can feel like gigantic leaps, but sometimes you simply have to take baby steps, my friends. Baby steps.

———

A pioneer in underground research of applied bioelectronic husbandry, Dr. Katzenstuff has been largely ignored by contemporary biographers. *Memoirs* is an effort to right this incalculable wrong.*

*no animals were harmed in the making of this work

———

Zandra Renwick's fiction has been translated into nine languages, performed on stage, and optioned for television. She writes in a triangulated midpoint between Portland (Oregon), Austin (Texas), and the heart of Canada's capital city (Ottawa). More at zandrarenwick.com.

SMUDGE

An essay by the daughter of Hershel Conway,
as provided by Jane Abbott

My father was called a crazy man. More than that—a mad scientist. Although I considered such terms to be insults, I admittedly never protested their validity. I never found the heart to blame anyone to think of him as such. Father always had ludicrous ideas and theories, and he was never afraid to share them with anyone—not even those who didn't possess the genius intellect to understand him.

Seeing that I was one such girl of average intelligence, Father spent hours on end thinking of how to explain his fantasies to a child. He often succeeded in doing so. Every lesson became a story that drew me further and further into the fantastic realm of science. These tales were mostly focused around astrophysics, a topic that sounded infinitely more drab and dull when coming out of the mouth of anyone else. Father was a genius in this regard, a master of entertainment. I enjoyed every lecture except one: the time travel demonstration.

It began on a warm July's day. I was reading a picture book about insects. My left elbow had been scraped badly due to a combination of poor balance and a bicycle that lacked training wheels. Father had patched me up, made me a peanut butter sandwich, and set the book in front of my face to dry my tears. About a half hour later, when the sandwich had been eaten and I had made my way to page 36, Father rushed to my side with a jar of water and a piece of paper. Seeing the smile on his face, I followed protocol and put my book down.

"How do you travel through time?" he asked. I blinked in confusion before answering:

"I don't know."

"Think simply. Just guess."

"You ... build a machine?"

"Exactly!" Father took a seat to my right. He lay the paper on the counter. Then he plucked a large paintbrush from his coat pocket, as well as a red pen. "You could call it a machine, but I'd call it more of an invention. I've named it Chronomorphium. It's a tool that will allow us to move forward in time. Isn't it neat?"

It most certainly was neat. Father drew a small dot in the upper left corner of the paper. "This," he said, "is us. Our world. And this"—he tapped his pen against the jar of water—"is Chronomorphium."

"Really?" I asked in wonder.

"No, not actually. This is water, but it represents Chronomorphium." Father dipped the paintbrush into it. "The paper is the universe as we know it. The farther right we go, the farther in time we are. For example, if we go here, just an inch or two to the right, we'd travel, oh, maybe a few years in the future. If we go across the page, we'd go quite a bit far ahead. Perhaps even by a thousand years."

Father slid the wet brush across the corner. He blew on it, fanning his hand at the same time to dry it faster. The corner began to rise and curl. I'd seen that happen many times before whenever I tried to paint. Father placed his middle fingertip onto the counter and his index finger to the corner of the paper, right over the red dot.

"This is where we once were," he said, bending his middle finger. Carefully, he made a little mark on the paper where the red dot hovered over. "This is where we are now. With a bit of Chronomorphium, we can travel a short distance. Do you follow?"

I nodded intently.

He picked up his brush, dipped it again, and swept it across the inside of the curl multiple times. The corner curled even further. Father marked his progress again with another scarlet mark. "Now we're even farther forward in time!"

"Can I try?" I asked, reaching for the jar.

"Wait, I'm not done yet." He picked up his jar of water. He swished the liquid around for a moment, studying it intently, before pouring it out on the corner.

I yanked my book to safety, staring at him with anger and confusion.

His eyes weren't on me, though. They were on the corner of the paper, which had turned into a messy pulp. The ink had run and smudged.

I looked at the mess, then at the carpet where the water had begun to drip to.

"Will you pick the corner up for me, please?"

I gingerly pinched the corner between my thumb and finger. The water was cold to the touch, almost frigid. The paper felt fragile, thin, and grainy. As I tugged on it as gently as I could, it ripped without a sound. I held the mushy corner to my face. The ink of the red dot had spread to the entire corner, turning it a faded pink. The world on the page had been distorted and destroyed.

"That is exactly why we must be careful when fooling around with such an unexplored concept such as time," Father stated. "No one knows what kind of paper our universe is made out of. It could be thick like cardstock or cardboard, or it could be thinner than a tissue."

Perhaps it was my ignorance to a bigger picture that caused me to pay no mind to the paper. I didn't care about the rip in the universe so much as what had become of the world. Father must have seen my vacant expression, because he gave me a rough pat on the back.

"Don't you worry," he bellowed cheerfully. "We would never use so much Chronomorphium. We are scientists. We are far more calculated than that. I was simply putting on a show for you. Do you want to try it?"

"No, thank you." I didn't mean to whisper.

Father took me out for ice cream after that, as well as a walk in the park. Although the demonstration had never left my mind, I pretended that it did for his sake. I loved Father, quite as he may have been at times. At a subconscious level, my farce of well-being was a small part of a debt I owed him for his kindness and patience with me. I knew of the antisocial, isolated nature that often came packaged with a scientific mind. A man with a personality like that would never make a good father, it seemed. I was lucky among children of geniuses. Father fed me, played with me, and loved me, all while maintaining his reputation as a pioneer to astrophysical science. The least I could do was assure him that I was alright.

My dream that night was very odd. Though I feel it would be a bit dramatic to label it as a nightmare, its content was disturbed enough to leave me feeling tired and uneasy the following morning. While I slept, I dreamed of myself in the kitchen, engrossed in my insect book. I heard the familiar footsteps of Father approaching. He called my name, and I turned to him. His face had turned into an unsettling smear. Father's features no longer stuck out as they should on a human. They were blurred and crude. I woke right then and there, my heart pounding as though it was trying to free itself of its ribcage.

In a few years' time, Father's application for a test trial of Chronomorphium was approved and funded. A child no longer, I frequently conversed with him about his studies. By this point in my life, time travel had consumed his. He kept a calendar hung on the wall and marked each passing day with a red X. The day of the trial, April 11th, grew nearer and nearer. When it finally arrived, Father hugged and kissed me goodbye. He promised to be back at the end of the day, but the look in his eyes suggested the possibility of a broken vow. He knew as much as I did about what kind of paper the universe was made of. He knew as well as I did whether he'd be back. I followed the protocol I had taken on since that July day: offer him a confident smile.

He took it, thanked me, and left.

I poured a cup of tea for him in the evening. I drank mine and poured myself another. I watched the steam from his dissipate into nothingness. The following morning, I dumped Father's cup into the sink and made more tea. This time, I left it in the kettle so it would keep its heat longer. Just as I expected, he never came back, nor did any of the others directly involved in the experiment.

Only a day later, the earth shook, and the tea I'd made for him crashed to the floor. From my window, I watched in horror as the houses I grew up playing around crumbled down into nothingness, then the buildings nestled in the heart of the city, then the rest of the world. Day by day, the remainders of humanity fled to what they prayed to be safety, desperate for asylum from the oncoming apocalypse. With every tsunami, fissure, tornado, and hurricane came the curse against my father from the survivors. Scientific explanation had abandoned us, just as my poor mad scientist had abandoned me for his dreams.

Only my home still stands against the rubble of everything. No one knows that the deathbringer's daughter shivers inside, pondering how long until the cold takes her life as well. I cannot argue against their outrage. There's no doubt in my mind that this sudden end was a consequence of his reckless actions. He bent the fabric of the universe, and the universe bent back. Perhaps in that same ripple of the universe's revenge, our planet was ripped apart at the seams, damned to break until nothing is left but bits and pieces floating in empty space. We are small, after all, and more fragile than we could ever imagine. With one scientific achievement, our entire being has collapsed.

As I lay dying in my bed, I can only think of my father, who I'm sure is dead as well. I can only hope that his death was no worse than ours—that he went out of existence in the blink of an eye. He most likely has been broken, too, stretched so far apart as he jumped through time that he's been reduced to nothing but a sheet of atoms floating in space, an unrecognizable smudge in the universe.

Hershel Conway was born the evening of July 8, 2045, in Glasgow, Scotland. A man with endless curiosity and unlimited genius, he quickly became an icon of science to the rest of the world. His first invention, the "Manipulator," which solidified small quantities of dark matter into tangible substance, landed him as a household name for generations to come. Though Conway's life was one of exploration and accomplishment, it wasn't without its grimmer moments. Conway's wife of four years, Sherri Blake, filed for divorce in 2071, leaving her heartbroken ex-husband to care for their young daughter. Rumors speculate that the stress of being left on his own to care for the child whose mother no longer loved him drove Conway to more macabre areas of interest, such as his expedition to revive animal subjects by "resuscitating their brain matter, segregating it from the dead flesh, and connecting it to an interface that could record any signs of intelligence." His request for a grant was immediately denied. He then moved on to less heavier subjects such as the possibility to travel forward in time. Conway's discovery of what he called Chronomorphium landed him once again in a positive light. Some scientists did little to contain their excitement at his approved plan for testing it, while others worried for his safety. The first experiment involving human life will take place on April 11, 2083. Only time will tell if this trial gives humanity a new way to travel through the universe.

Jane Abbott was born in 1999. Since an early age, she's lived in Spokane, Washington. This is the first of a hopefully long list of publications for her. Her love of science-fiction was heavily inspired by video games like the *Metroid* series and the *Alien* movie franchise. Jane currently attends Spokane Falls Community College and hopes to become an author as well as a creative writing teacher.

TIME AND AGAIN

An essay by an unnamed assistant,
as provided by Stephen D. Rogers

First of all, it wasn't my fault. And even if it were my fault, it was an accident. I never meant to bend time into a Mobius strip, and probably couldn't have done that if I tried. Besides, what kind of idiot tries to manipulate the physics of cause and effect?

My kind of idiot.

Let's just get this straight: it wasn't my experiment, it wasn't my theory, and it wasn't my idea.

This human of mine, he gets these flashes of stupidity that he mistakes for brilliance, and unfortunately, he knows just enough science to follow through.

Who gets blamed for the mishaps? Right, me.

I'm always there—as if I had any choice—and so I'm automatically at fault.

You might think that perhaps my human would take some responsibility for errors. Ha! He takes the credit when things go well, and everything else is on me. That's just how he is.

If I had any say in the matter, I'd be gone in a flash.

To be completely honest, I'm surprised there hasn't been a mistake of this magnitude before now.

The laboratory is a mess. Things all over the place. Would it kill him to put something away for once?

But no, he just leaves the uncapped bottle of water next to the open control box, circuits exposed, nothing shielded. It's as if he wanted me to knock the bottle over.

Before I begin, I just want you to understand that it's not my fault. To make a long story short: I've got this shadow, this invisible manifestation, that I just can't shake loose.

It's a curse. The curse of the transparent assistant.

I'm sure you can appreciate how difficult it is for me to accomplish important work when I've got this ... thing ... hovering. How could anyone in their right mind expect me to concentrate?

Quite simply, the situation is intolerable. Intolerable and yet I tolerate it. But why must I tolerate it?

I was a scientist. Scientists discover solutions. That's what we do.

Then I got this brilliant idea. What if I jiggered time? What if I leapt backward or forward a few tiny milliseconds? That shock to the continuum might just be enough to break whatever bond connected me to my ghost, leaving me free to go about my work without interference.

I would use science to endow science, the first allowing the second, the second empowering the first, an infinite loop of enlightened development.

The thrill of expectation lifted the weight that had clouded my mind, enabling me to achieve one breakthrough after another until I defeated the tyranny of time.

Take that, you invisible fiend! Take that, you fraud!

And then that creature, calculating and vindictive, poured a bottle of water into the fragile mechanism that controlled my invention.

I watched everything I worked for go up in smoke.

First of all, it wasn't my fault. And even if it were my fault, it was an accident. I never meant to bend time into a Mobius strip, and probably couldn't have done that if I tried.

What does Rogers mean by "Made-up Languages"? I speak three of them. Am I made up? Definitely not. Maybe I should write *An Encyclopedia of Imaginary Writers*. Maybe I'll do that. Maybe I'll do that and send him a copy, and then once I have his address, I'll write an *Atlas of Make-Believe Locations*.

See how he likes that. Hmph.

Stephen D. Rogers is the author of *A Dictionary of Made-Up Languages* and more than 800 shorter pieces. His website, www.StephenDRogers.com, includes a list of new and upcoming titles as well as other timely information.

THE SKITTERER: AN IMPRESSION OF AN IMAGINARY COMPANION

An essay by Titus Rodriguez, Ph.D.,
as provided by G. D. Watry

Abstract: For decades, myriad parapsychologists have pondered the role of so-called "imaginary companions" (IC) in cases concerning poltergeist activity. Though we may theorize the rhyme and reason for it, children appear to amplify the poltergeist presence. Indeed, our own lab's case studies, localized to the northwest pocket of New Jersey, indicate a positive correlation between quantifiable poltergeist activity and the presence of a child or children in the studied household.

In our experience, the events follow a trajectory. New occupants move into the house and an IC manifests. It induces interaction with the child or children. Cumulative contact appears to be key here, for each interaction strengthens the psychic bond between IC and adolescent/s. We've termed this relationship "cerebral parasitism," and its effects are not limited to the psychological. Physical illness and disturbances often follow. Poltergeist activity crescendos. Pranks that were once innocuous turn perilous, and occupants often report experiencing psychological and physical torment at the behest of unseen beings. The Mayfield family may have been such a case.

Gwen Mayfield contacted the Rodriguez Lab on the morning of March 19, 2015, following what she believed to be a botched abduction of her son Tobias by an entity she called "the skitterer." Ms. Mayfield and her son had recently moved into a new house at 8474 La Vela Avenue in the Borough of Sussex on March 14, 2015, following a falling out with her partner Arnold Recker, a known affiliate of The Coyote Moon (SEE INDEX ITEM "COYOTE MOON, THE; CULT"). The Coyote Moon boasts strong membership in the Borough of Sussex region, with members of the commune active in both municipal and policing roles.

After contact, the team performed an exploratory interview with Ms. Mayfield on March 21, 2015. The following is an audio transcript from that interview, which ended, to our displeasure, in an abrupt manner. Unfortunately, we were unable to schedule a follow-up interview with Ms. Mayfield. She and her three-year-old son Tobias disappeared. They were last seen by their neighbor Mrs. Lupe Galvan on the night of March 22, 2015. Mrs. Galvan recalled seeing the mother and child sitting silently in their backyard, "their hands clasped together as if in prayer and their heads upturned in deference towards the moon."

We are at a loss, and this is an appeal for assistance.

~

[Selections from the audio transcript of Dr. Titus Rodriguez's interview with Gwen Mayfield on March 21, 2015]

TR: And that's when you noticed the crib was empty?

GM: H-he, he just wasn't there anymore. I must've shut my eyes for just a second, but that's all it took. One second, I'm lost in the grainy light from the baby monitor app on my iPhone, watching Tobe's body rise and fall with his breath, and the next, I'm jolted awake, kicking back the grip of sleep, and he's gone. The crib is empty, and he's gone.

TR: And what did you do next?

GM: What did I do next? Jesus. You're not a parent are you, doc?

TR: [No response.]

GM: I shot out of bed and looked like hell for him is what I did next. Nearly broke my ankle slipping on the hallway's Persian carpet while sprinting to his room.

TR: Was he in there?

GM: What? No, no he wasn't in there. Are you even listening?

TR: Apologies, Ms. Mayfield. I am listening. Continue.

GM: The crib was empty, but the jungle mobile above it played its jingle, a toy piano version of "Ring Around the Rosy." The mobile activates via motion sensors, so something must've kicked it into gear. But it wasn't Tobe. I'm sure of that. For a moment, I couldn't move. I just stood there, watching the plush lions chase the monkeys round and round the four-leaf canopy. When I originally bought the mobile, I thought it was cute. But two nights ago, it just seemed—fierce. The lions bared their teeth, and the monkeys—oh, god—their faces. [Long pause.]

TR: How long did it take you to find Tobias in the driveway?

GM: [Sniffs. Coughs.] Probably 20 minutes. I tore the house apart; I mean, it's not big a place, so there aren't many places to look, and we're practically still living out of boxes. I was checking again for him under the kitchen table when I noticed the door to the garage was open. Through the crack in the door, I could see the lawn lights from the house across the street.

TR: Why were you looking for Tobias under the kitchen table?

GM: It's his favorite spot for hide-and-seek.

TR: Was it unusual that the door to the garage was open?

GM: Very. I always keep it locked. All the doors actually. Ever since the incident with Arnold.

TR: And that would be Arnold Recker?

GM: Yes, but as I said on the phone, we're not discussing that.

TR: [No response.]

GM: Anyway, the next thing I know, I'm bounding through the garage, my mind swimming with visions of Tobe's picture on the morning news, of pedestrians checking their phones in unison as an amber alert hits their inboxes. I don't think I've ever screamed so loud. [Pause.] My mom always says I shouldn't be a parent. [Long pause.]

TR: He was still there, Ms. Mayfield. You didn't lose him.

GM: I almost did. I think I am. [Crying.]

TR: Ms. Mayfield, can you tell me what happened next?

GM: [Sniffs.] It's like you said; he wasn't gone. As soon as I peeled out into the moonlight, I saw him on the driveway. He sat in this strange position, almost like an obedient dog. I scooped him up as quickly as I could and hugged him to me tight. My little monkey. He felt limp in my grip, and I held him out by the shoulders, just to give him a once over. His head teetered, and his eyes rolled in their sockets. He looked dazed, like a drunk. That's when I noticed his teeth were chattering and that his pajamas were damp with sweat. He collapsed in my arms almost immediately.

Before he passed out, he said, "Mommy, the skitterer says I can be a monster too."

TR: And who's the skitterer?

GM: Tobe's imaginary friend.

TR: [Mumbling.] Ms. Mayfield, I hate to interrupt, but my colleague tells me our audio equipment is experiencing some technical difficulties.

GM: Have you been recording any of this?

TR: Only partially.

BREAK IN RECORDING

TR: You noticed the discharge from his ears this morning?

GM: Yes, it was all gunky. White like bird shit, but thick like typical ear wax, and this stuff had specks of black and red in it too. I noticed it because Tobe's got Bear in the Big Blue House crib sheets.

TR: If it's possible, we'd like to get a sample of that for analysis. Where is Tobias now?

GM: [Pause.] He's with my mom. She's taking care of him.

TR: Would it be possible for us to see him?

GM: [Long pause.] You got that thing running now?

TR: [Coughs.] 1, 2—1, 2, 3, 4. Yes, we are recording. Would you like anything more before we start? Water?

GM: I'm fine.

TR: Okay. Ms. Mayfield, can you walk me through the incidents leading up to the night of March 18?

GM: You mean the freaky shit?

TR: Yes, the freaky shit.

GM: It started with little things pretty much from the first day we moved in. Tobe was outside playing in the front yard while I set up his room. A chainlink fence surrounds our lawn, so I wasn't worried about him tumbling out into Route 15 traffic. Anyway, I'm a smoker, so after setting up his crib, I wanted to reward myself with a puff from the vape pen. I always keep it handy in my front shirt pocket, but when I reached for it, I came up empty-handed.

TR: And as you mentioned on the phone, you found the vape pen—

GM: I'm getting to it, doc. Jeez. Well, after some fruitless searching, I decided to delve into my backup pack of cigarettes.

Figured I'd have one outside. It'd give me a moment to check in on Tobe. When I stepped out onto the deck, Tobe was sitting on the bench swing. That's when I saw it. My vape pen was right next to him on the wooden bench. It struck me as odd, because I definitely would've heard Tobe enter the house. Our alarm system is one those ones that announces actions in a halting manner, like "Close. Front. Door." And I definitely would've noticed Tobe stealing my vape pen. I may wear thick specs, but I ain't blind. Anyway, Tobe blamed the skitterer. He said my lungs were filled with tar.

TR: That's the other thing I wanted to ask, Tobias has become more vocal recently, hasn't he? Since his encounter with the skitterer?

GM: That's right. He's always been a quiet child. But recently, he started talking more. Not really words—well if they're words, they're not of the English variety. I'll catch him in his room babbling incoherencies to empty space. He pauses too, like he's in the midst of a conversation with someone and waiting for their reply. His drawings have changed too. He always used to draw stick figure equivalents of pastoral landscapes, with bright crayons smeared across the page. But lately, black's been his favorite color. And what he draws—I think it's the view of the surrounding woods from our backyard, but there's always something hidden among the trees, the same figure. At first, it starts off as floating eyes in the wood, but the drawings are sequential, see. In each new picture, the figure inches closer and closer to our house. Long-limbed and waxing, it always looks as if it's rising above the forest, its snouted face as luminous as the moon.

TR: This is the skitterer.

GM: That's what I assume.

TR: [Mumbling.] —what I'm telling you is I don't think we need to rush it.

GM: Everything alright?

TR [Mumbling.] —I understand; fine. Ms. Mayfield, can you tell us about your association with Mr. Recker? Is he Tobe's father?

GM: [Pause.] Thought I said we weren't gonna talk about him.

TR: Please, Ms. Mayfield, just follow my thoughts for a moment. My team and I, we're familiar with Mr. Arnold Recker. He's actually been on our radar for quite some time.

GM: That exit sign above your head gets greener with every word, Doc.

TR: Just wait. We know about his membership in The Coyote Moon's high council.

GM: [No response.]

TR: We also know that up until the start of this month, you and your son lived in one of the cabins on The Coyote Moon commune's property, near Liminal Lake. Let me be frank, Ms. Mayfield, there's been a pattern, one that concerns me and my colleagues. Since The Coyote Moon's arrival in the Borough of Sussex, there's been a surge in poltergeist activity in the region.

GM: Poltergeist? [Sound of metal chair grating against tile floor.] Boy, you eggheads really are out of your depth with this one, aren't you? To think I thought y'all could help me. [Sound of footsteps. Sound of door opening.]

TR: Please, Ms. Mayfield, something's happening. We'd be grateful for any light you can shed on The Coyote Moon for us.

GM: [Muffled.] Unfortunately for you, Doc, I don't control the light of the moon. And neither do you.

TR: Fuck. [Pause.] I told you we shouldn't push it.

END OF TRANSCRIPT

~

Postscript: By publishing this transcript we hope to spark some recognition in at least one of *Mad Scientist Journal*'s readers. Gwen Mayfield was right to say my colleagues and I are out of our depth on this case. We utterly are. Since the disappearance of Gwen and Tobias, each of my team members has been plagued by the same dream of an impossibly tall creature loping high above the forest in the middle of the night. Those of us with children have noticed shifts in their behavior. Just this morning, my seven-year-old daughter approached me—her gait rigid, her face catatonic—with a new picture she drew for our refrigerator. The creature's limbs are so long. I have no doubt it can reach into our houses. Below the cartoon image, my daughter wrote a caption: "The skitterer says we can be monsters too."

Titus Rodriguez, Ph.D., is a research scientist at a stealth startup in the Hudson Valley. Before jumping to industry, he was a faculty member at

The Barron Institute's Center for Cognitive Psychology and Behavioral Neuroscience.

G. D. Watry is a writer from California. His work has appeared in *Pantheon Magazine*, *Hinnom Magazine*, *OCCULUM*, *Shotgun Honey*, Third Flatiron Publishing, and *The Molotov Cocktail*, among other publications. You can find him on Twitter @GDWatry.

DISINHIBITED

An excerpt from the journals of Combat Search & Rescue
Consultant Lana McGee, as provided by Myna Chang

―――――――

Don't call me a mercenary. Those guys are pricks. Kidnappers and murderers, the lot of them. I'm not like that. Sure, I get paid for my work, and yeah, I love a good explosion. Who doesn't? But my job is to save people. Pull them out of bad situations. Bring them home safe.

I'm not an asshole.

"I didn't think you were, Ma'am."

Oh shit, did I say all that out loud?

"Yes, Ma'am, you did."

Wow, this pilot doesn't look old enough to shave, let alone fly a chopper.

"I shave, Ma'am."

"You heard that, too?"

"Yes, Ma'am. My CO warned me this might happen."

"Name's Lana, not Ma'am. So, they told you about my disability?" *Their word, not mine.*

"They said you got a piece of shrapnel in your head. War souvenir. Said you blurt out whatever crosses your mind."

"Yep," I nod. "Frontal Lobe Disinhibition. Basically, if I think it, I say it. That's why I'm freelancing now."

"Yes, Ma'am. Not a merc. Got it."

Pilot's quick. And he does shave. Sexy stubble. Yum. Like to run my tongue up that jawline and—

"Due respect, Ma'am, I'm authorized to tell you to shut up."

I bite my rogue tongue hard enough to draw blood. *Damn it, Lana. Stop scaring the cute flyboy.*

He flicks his eyes toward me and grins. "Truth is, Ma'am, I don't scare easy."

Oh. Well, then. I smile and shift in the seat. "Just to be clear ... You wouldn't mind—"

"Approaching the drop zone, Ma'am."

I chuckle. His smile turns to a blush. *Tease.* "Fine, kick me out of your helicopter. Come on, Diamond, we've got people to rescue."

My German Shepherd sits while I attach a jump harness to her K-9 armor. Takes about three seconds. We've done hundreds of these short jumps, and it never gets old. She woofs, ready to go.

"Godspeed."

"You talking to me or the dog?"

"Both of you, Ma'am."

He maneuvers the chopper over the moonlit compound and flashes a cheeky grin at me again. I try to keep my mouth shut, but as usual, the words tumble out.

"I'm probably gonna lick your stubbly jaw when this mission's over, Pilot. Diamond might, too."

"Countin' on it, Ma'am."

I laugh and step into the air.

~

The research facility sits on a swath of blacktop, devoid of plant life, a big wart on a bald head. The gate hangs open. I toss a handful of debris at the razor-wire fence, but it doesn't spark. Looks like the power's out. Not a good sign.

I was hoping this job would be a quickie: rescue the dashing scientist, secure his peculiar research, get home in time for dinner. Guess I should've known better. Anything involving Chase Mathews isn't going to be easy.

"At least the compound hasn't been bombed yet, huh girl?"

Diamond doesn't respond. She's good like that.

A Jeep sits abandoned near the fence. Wet-looking handprints smear the windshield, and a case of medical supplies has toppled onto the asphalt.

We skirt it, watching for movement, hoping for some sign of life as we approach the entrance. Nothing stirs. I tighten my grip on the MTAR submachine gun strapped across my chest, and we enter the facility.

Lobby's dark, except for orange warning lights at the guard's terminal. My NVGs flare in time with the flashes, so I pull them off. Diamond's night vision is more reliable than the goggles, anyway. She's the most capable combat partner I've worked with; I trust her with my life.

She nudges me. I nod, and she ghosts away, into the darkness. Nothing will get past her. A low growl, five yards to the right, alerts me to an enemy combatant. I bring my MTAR to bear, just in time. Two quick bursts, and the bad guy goes down.

I love this fucking gun. Compact and efficient, with a little kick. Kind of like me.

Diamond circles the lobby, vigilant, then returns to my side. I prod the body splayed in front of me. Scrawny dude, white lab coat. Blisters all over his face.

Or are those pustules? Jesus, that's nasty looking. Diamond keens and backs away. I follow her lead. A blister-thing quavers and ruptures, spurting out thick goo. Hard to tell in the darkness, but I think it's green.

I'll never eat lime Jell-O again. Diamond rubs her head on my thigh; she won't either.

"Come on, girl. Our dashing scientist isn't going to rescue himself."

She snorts her disapproval. Diamond had never liked Chase. She'd peed on his shoes every chance she got. My dog's smart. I should have listened.

~

We creep down the hallway behind the guard station. Emergency lights flicker, strobing the corridor in snapshots of weirdness.

Flash. Body on the floor.

Flash. Smear of blood.

Flash. Heap of clothing, soaked with green sludge.

I wish the freakin' light would either stay on or go dark. Vertigo pulses with every disco blink.

Diamond lets out a cautionary rumble, and I pull up my gun, ready to fire. A woman covered in angry boils slumps on the floor, back against the wall. She reaches out blindly, hands grasping air.

My first-aid kit's in my pack, but I'm not ready to take my finger off the trigger guard; Diamond's hackles are still up. The woman's mouth opens and tainted saliva gushes out. Looks like pond scum.

I don't think my emergency band-aids will do you much good, lady.

She jerks toward my voice, moaning. Spit froths on her lips. Several of her boils burst, popping like firecrackers, loud enough I can hear them over my thundering heartbeat. Syrupy goop, smelling of burnt licorice, oozes from the sores. Her body cants sideways and her shoulder hits the floor.

Nothing I can do will help her now. Maybe we'll find a miracle cure in the lab. Diamond and I hug the far side of the hallway, avoiding her still-seeking arms. The thick fluids pooling around her body seem to throb in time with the emergency lights, and the cloying odor intensifies as we pass.

I'm not sure what we've gotten ourselves into, but I sure hope this bug isn't airborne. Our combat armor should protect us from physical contaminants, but it doesn't do anything to block out the stink.

We come to a junction. I remember the blueprints and hang a left. The bulb in this hallway's dim, but at least it's not blinking. Unfortunately, the path is blocked by a mass of writhing bodies.

All naked—explains the abandoned clothes back there—dotted with throbbing cysts. Many have already ruptured, leaving curdled trails of emerald slime. I stare, fascinated. The people are fusing together; everywhere the goo touches, their skin melds. Limbs, feet, heads, all merging into one giant blob.

Diamond paws the floor. One of the faces snaps up, focusing its attention on her. We back away. A distorted jaw juts out, leering. It trembles, and a body begins to emerge from the fused clump of flesh, first a shoulder, then a torso. Straining to reach us, it makes a squelching slurp and tears free—an arm, two legs.

The legs don't match.

My stomach turns. The newly assembled monster stumbles and lurches at Diamond.

I shoot it in the head. It stops, but doesn't fall, so I pop it again, center mass, where a heart and lungs should be. It totters for a split second before collapsing.

Diamond whines; the rest of the entangled mound of creatures squirms toward us. Maybe the gunfire got its—their?—attention. They stretch and heave, inching closer. Unnatural liquids gurgle and flesh splits as they rip themselves apart, rubbery appendages groping relentlessly in Diamond's direction.

I flip the toggle on my MTAR to full auto and spray the clusterfuck. No way in hell those abominations are gonna get sticky with my pup. I let up on the trigger and watch for movement, then give them another blast, just to be sure.

I guess a full magazine was enough to do the job, which is good because, damn, that's a scary pile of monsters. But now the hallway's coated in weird-colored gore. Not gonna risk going through that mess. Doesn't matter, though. According to the map, all hallways lead to the inner lab, where the research stuff should be stored.

And Chase. Can't forget him, the handsome, charming scientist. My ex.

~

The electronic lock is toast and the lab door won't open. Something's wedged it shut. I kick it, hard, but that only hurts my foot.

"Chase? Are you in there?" *Hope he's not glued to the mishmash back in the hallway.*

Diamond watches my back while I pound on the reinforced steel.

"Lana? Is that you?"

"Yeah, and I wanna see if you still turn me on." *Damn it.*

"Are you infected?"

"I can still talk, can't I?" *Of course I can. It's my biggest problem.*

The door cracks open. He squints at me.

"Why'd they send you?"

"No one else'd take the job." *True story.*

Diamond and I squeeze through the door and shove it closed again.

"Did you bring a platoon of Marines to save me?" Chase demands.

I spread my arms. "Just us."

He groans.

Not as charming as I remember.

"If you're all they sent," he says, "they're going to nuke the whole island, aren't they?"

"Probably. I figure we've got another hour before the bombing starts."

"No, no, no, it's too valuable," he mutters, already ignoring me.

Feels like old times.

His motions are jerky. He grabs a backpack and shoves miniature computer drives and scraps of paper into it.

Definitely not a turn-on anymore. Looks like hell, all bug-eyed and twitchy. Kinda soft around the edges.

He stops and glares at me.

Stinks, too.

"Still the motor-mouthed bitch."

Oops. "I didn't mean—"

"Yeah, you did. You've always been an asshole. The piece of shrapnel just makes it more obvious."

That hurts. Gotta admit it. A muffled thud from the hallway preempts my snarky response. Diamond snarls, low and intense. The warning tone sends goosebumps up my spine.

"Chase, what happened to those people?"

He shrugs. "Sample got out. Spread a lot faster than I expected."

"Sample? The research I'm supposed to retrieve?"

"Thought you were here to rescue me."

"Yeah, but boss-man said you're low priority. 'Get the research,' he said. 'Grab the scientist, too, if you can.' That's what he said."

"God, I hate the military," Chase spits.

I have to agree, at least a little. CO didn't mention the rest of the research staff. Guess the woman in the hall is zero-priority in his book. I call bullshit on that—I'll save whoever I can.

"Is there a cure, or an antidote?"

"Why?" he asks, backing away from me. "Did you get any of the transfer medium on you?"

"You mean the green goo? No. But maybe some of the others are still alive."

He goes back to rifling through the science junk on his desk. "I only make the contagions. Cures are someone else's department."

Seriously? "So you're a full-on mad scientist now?"

"I prefer bioweapon engineer."

I stare at him. *Has he always been this cold-hearted?*

Diamond barks, two short yips. *That's a yes.*

Chase rolls his eyes and I realize I've spoken out loud again. He glares at Diamond.

"Bitch."

"You talking to me or the dog?"

"What do you think?" He shoulders past me, opening a biohazard safe. Polished steel containers crowd the shelf. They look like those expensive vacuum insulated tumbler thingies. He yanks one out.

"You keep your weaponized slime in a fancy coffee cup?"

He sneers and shoves the container into the backpack. "I can't believe they sent a brain damaged mercenary to rescue me."

That's 'value-priced consultant' to you, jerkface. Diamond snarls, exposing her fangs.

"Can you both shut up?" His hands shake.

Wait. Faster than he expected? How did the sample get out?

"A test," he answers. "Proof of concept for the buyer."

"You infected those people on purpose? So you can sell that stuff?"

He laughs. "You weren't very smart, even before the shrapnel." He zips his pack and turns.

Something's wrong with his face.

Diamond's growl modulates into a high-pitched howl—her extreme danger signal. Almost too late, I realize why: Chase is infected. I didn't see it before. Hard to miss now.

I raise my MTAR. A smudge of emerald gel shimmers on the edge of the safe behind him. "Don't move."

He gapes at me, incredulous. "Put the gun down, Lana."

I shake my head. "You must've gotten sloppy with your death jelly."

"How dare you?" He frowns and scratches at a freshly blossoming pustule on his right cheek. His fingers drip green. "No!"

Diamond moves into a defensive position, guarding me. Chase stares dumbly at his stained hand. He raises frightened eyes to mine.

"Lana, help me."

My gun barrel wavers. Diamond barks, short and sharp, warning him to stay back, reminding me to follow protocol. Chase reaches out to me.

"Please—" His voice devolves into a mewl. Sanity, whatever's left of it, drains from his eyes. His face morphs, cheeks melting in a slurry of jade-colored paste. Pus drips from his scalp. He screams and launches himself at me, and for the first time in my professional career, I freeze.

But Diamond doesn't.

She meets him mid-air, bashing into him with her shoulder. She ricochets off his body, crashing to the floor a few feet from where he lands. Teeth bared, she's up in an instant, but he's already charging toward her, crablike, faster than I've ever seen him move.

Diamond! Don't bite him!

I don't know if I've screamed or if she's read my mind, but she keeps her mouth off him. We slide into a familiar rhythm of charge and retreat, strike and evade. She dodges, giving me a clear shot. I squeeze the trigger. Chase's head explodes.

Clabbered wet tissue splatters across his desk. Ears ringing, I inch closer and nudge the slack body, but it doesn't move. His entire head is gone. I doubt anything could survive that, but I give him a double tap, two to the chest, to be safe. Then I drop the gun and rush to Diamond.

You stupid dog. Did the goo splash you? I run my hands over her armor, up and down her legs, check her mouth and her teeth. After examining her doggie armpits for the second time, my panic dissipates. She's okay; the K-9 gear did its job. She nuzzles my face, and I realize she's cleaning up my tears. I wrap my arms around her, trembling. *Good girl.*

~

I call for evac and wait for the thump of chopper blades to split the air.

On a normal mission, I'd feel rotten about failing to bring my target home alive. This time, not so much. I drag a clean duffel behind me. It's filled with Chase's notes and computer drives, but not the bio sample. I left that crap behind for the bombs to take care of.

The chopper circles. I flash my light, three quick blinks, and it lands.

"Look, Diamond, it's the yummy pilot."

She woofs and thumps her tail.

"Oh, you approve of this one?"
She barks twice; that's a *yes*.
"Okay then, let's go give him a lick."

─────────

Combat Search & Rescue Consultant Lana McGee specializes in the retrieval of personnel and property from high-risk environments. McGee is assisted by a Hero-Class German Shepherd named Diamond. McGee has recently raised her consultation fees, and now charges a premium for any "mad scientist bullshit."

─────────

Myna Chang writes flash and short stories. Her work has been featured in *Daily Science Fiction*, *The Copperfield Review*, *Defenestration*, and *Dead Housekeeping*, among others. Find her @MynaChang or read more at mynachang.com.

THE EXPERIMENT MEETS CERTAIN DOOM

An essay by Experiment 105, as related by Deborah L. Davitt

I looked up from inside my cage as the skylight of the laboratory opened, and blinked. A swarm of insects poured through the opening, coalescing near the floor. The insects seethed, never entirely outlining the form with perfect resolution, but I could interpolate the shape of a human female. One that now rooted among the cabinets, chucking tools into a sack.

"Excuse me," I said politely. Mother had taught me to *always* be polite. "You needn't steal. If you're hungry, Mother will give you food. She says everything she does is to help others."

The swarm dissolved. Reformed, the limbs melding front to back, the face melting through the back of the head to become the front. "Mother? She lets you call her that?" The voice sounded like the susurration of a million wings. "She didn't let me call her *Mother* even when I was her flesh-and-blood daughter."

I sat upright. "You're her *daughter?*"

"Once, yes." Insects billowed toward me, then curled back into human shape. "Until she tried to destroy me."

I hesitated. *Mother's good. Mother would never try to destroy anything that wasn't evil.* "Are you ... certain doom or something?"

"She named me Melissa, first. Then Swarm. Then, yes, Certain Doom. It has a ring, don't you think?"

"What *happened?*" I whispered, shocked.

"A period of mutual discovery. She discovered that most people didn't want to eat bugs. I discovered that *I* didn't want to be eaten by people. And people discovered that large swarms of insects often devour entire fields of grain. The local farmers drove her out of town. I followed, because she was my mother, and I didn't know anything else." A pause. "Like you and all the others."

I clutched the bars, half in panic, half in desperate hope. "There are others? Like us?"

Swarm continued packing tools. "A few. She always starts off with good intentions. Trying to solve some fundamental human problem. I started off as a way to prevent starvation. Famine. She couldn't afford to feed both of us, so why not make me experiment 17?"

I hesitated. I had faint memories of lean years. Hunger. But those memories weren't mine. "And the others?"

"She wanted a universal cure for disease. Built a clockwork doctor who could tirelessly nurse the sick. You know what they call him now?" She might've been staring at me. "The Plaguebringer. He has a few loose screws, but I get along with him."

My mouth fell open. "That's terrible."

"So was trying to *melt him down* after she gave him consciousness, instead of trying to fix him. I told him tonight I'd get him materials to repair his slagged feet." A gesture at the tools in the bag. "I figure 73 will do the trick."

"Then why's 87 in your sack? It's a death-ray."

Swarm undulated. "She shouldn't have 87. No one should, really." She turned away.

I hated the idea of losing her. The first person who'd really talked with me in ... ever. "Wait! Who else is there?"

Swarm turned back. "She adopted a little boy. Operated on his brain with Plaguebringer." A hiss of displeasure. "Gave him the ability to project thoughts."

"That doesn't sound terrible."

"She wanted him to help people not to fight. Noble ambition, except he could *hear* everyone around him. All the hatred, all the petty jealousies. He was only eight. It drove him insane." Swarm slumped, losing her shape for a moment. "So he made the voices *stop*. Killed them, or made them fight each other till they died. She tried to kill him, too. But I snatched him away. So now I have to steal food and clothes for him."

I didn't want to believe her. But I did.

Now Swarm floated closer. "You look *just* like her. Do you even remember being a child?"

"I *am* a child!"

56

"You have an adult body." Swarm's whispering voice sounded concerned. "You shouldn't let her treat you like this. Keep you in a cage."

It hadn't occurred to me that there were other options.

"You want out?"

I rattled the door. "How? It's locked!"

One of Swarm's hands billowed loose of her body. Buzzed to the keys on the far wall, then deposited them in my palm. Solid. Real. "If you want to meet the others, I can arrange it. One happy family."

"One would make me sick. And the other would just ... make me think you're right." My heart pounded. "He could be up on the roof, influencing me right now."

A rustle of laughter. "He's up there, sure. But he's not pushing you. Use your mind. You're a younger duplicate of her body. What human problem could you possibly be designed to solve for her?"

"She's been putting a cap on my head," I confessed, "while she wears another. Afterward, I have new thoughts. Memories that aren't mine. She tests to see how long I retain it."

Swarm seemed to nod. "Consciousness transfer. When she's satisfied that you retain information permanently, she'll transfer her mind into your body. Wiping *you* out." Swarm sighed. "She kills all her children, eventually. Why should you be any different?"

I licked my lips. "I don't want to be her."

"You don't want to *die*."

"That, either."

Swarm pointed at the key. "Your life's your own now." A pause. "So's hers." She poured back toward the skylight, carrying the sack.

I could bypass security. Get to Mother, kill her. Keep her from making more creatures like us. Or I could put the caps on both of us, and steal all Mother's knowledge. Become a better version of her.

Or I could leave Mother to the certain doom of her own mortality. And become the best version of *myself* I could be.

"Swarm! Take me with you!"

My sister boiled back down. Surrounded me. And carried me back out into the night sky, where our brothers awaited.

———

Experiment 105 believes that she's probably about ten to twelve years old, though rapid-maturation technology gives her the appearance of an adult human female. She didn't grab her mother's lab notes on her existence, however, so it's hard to tell precisely when she was decanted from her artificial womb. At some point in the future, she thinks that she might like to pick a name for herself. In the meantime, her siblings have taken to calling her Peri, which she thinks sounds like a chip from a paint store, but it's hard to argue with them, when they're the only family she's got.

Deborah L. Davitt was raised in Nevada, but currently lives in Houston, Texas, with her husband and son. Her poetry has received Rhysling, Dwarf Star, and Pushcart nominations; her short fiction has appeared in *InterGalactic Medicine Show*, *Compelling Science Fiction*, and *Pseudopod*. For more about her work, including her Edda-Earth novels and her poetry collection, *The Gates of Never*, please see www.edda-earth.com.

JEHOVAH'S FEATHERS

An essay by Mary Magdalene Farconi, as provided by K. Kitts

―――――――――

Strapped in his bouncy seat, my son Tyler went off at the exact same moment as the kitchen timer *and* the doorbell. I verified that nothing was actually gnawing on him and rushed to the brownies. Paul would have to get the door.

From the living room, Cissie yelled, "It's the bird people." Being a good girl, she knew not to open the door to strangers, especially those from another planet.

I yelled, "Paul, get the door," while I yanked the brownies from the oven.

The Home Owners Association bake sale started at 10 AM, and it was already 10:10. In my head, Mrs. Topher, the HOA president, admonished, "In *my* day, people respected each other and were on time."

As I dashed toward Tyler, I mumbled, "Yeah, back when Moses parted the Red Sea, most mothers of young children didn't have to analyze a 270-page watershed impact statement by Monday."

Before I unbuckled Tyler from his seat, I smelled his problem. The doorbell rang again. "Paul! Get the door!"

From the living room, Cissie yelled, "The bird people are still here."

I hustled down the hall with Tyler at arm's length. His room also served as Paul's home office. Sure enough. Paul had his earbuds in and was playing some computer game. I hip-butted the back of his chair.

Startled, he yelled, "What the—" but stopped in time. We try not to cuss like muleskinners in front of the kids. I handed Tyler over.

"I'm working, Maggie. You do it." He tried to pass Tyler back.

The doorbell rang a third time. Cissie called, "The bird people are *still* still here."

I said, "One, since when is slaying boss monsters a part of your job? And two, it's Saturday. We agreed on Saturdays you have to help. No questions asked." As I stomped to the front door, I muttered, "That is if you ever want to have sex again."

Hand on the knob, I breathed in deeply and exhaled. Bird people are sensitive. I didn't want to frighten them because they'd take off in a flurry of feathers and shrieks and dump whatever they had in their cloacas. I didn't have time to hose off the front porch.

I'd worked with several bird people when I'd served as an analyst for the newly established Alien Affairs Bureau. That was until the AAB's work rules changed and became intolerable for nursing moms. Two months after Tyler was born, I moved to a clean water non-profit with a short commute. The work wasn't as important, but my hair had stopped falling out. However, when I opened the door, I wondered whether I'd been out of the loop a little too long.

Instead of a group of sleek greenish-blue peacock-cranes, there stood two bedraggled and dull office drones dressed in modified white button-downs and khakis. Their tails were clipped and their wings pressed tightly against their backs. Even the frills on the tops of their heads drooped. They were both so dull in color, I couldn't tell whether they were male or female, but given the office casual, I guessed males.

Clutched in one of the T-Rex arms that protruded from beneath his breast, the left bird person held a black book. His colleague grasped a plastic sheet upon which text flickered.

I asked, "May I help you?"

Book bird bobbed his head and pressed the first icon on the squawk box on a chain around his neck. In a mellifluous voice, the box intoned, "Good morning! We are in your neighborhood seeking to expand our flock."

I frowned. If they were looking for females, they were out of luck. Our HOA categorically refused all building permits for aviaries. And with such poor color, I doubted any female would give them the time of day.

He cocked his head and pressed the second icon. The box asked, "Have you been saved by Jesus?"

I face-palmed. Flocking was extremely important to them. It made sense they'd become a target of some strip mall prophet, but where was their female, and why would she allow this to happen? "To which home nest do you belong?"

"Reverend Vernon P. Hogg," said the plastic paper bird. He passed the flickering sheet over.

The title read: *The Watch Perch.* The address running along the top was the old non-denominational church that had sold its parking lot to the highway extension.

Articles flitted past on how Jesus could save the faithful from obesity, drunkenness, and bird lice. "No, I mean your mother bird. Who is she?" I tried to return the plastic paper, but the bird refused to take it.

"Our Most Supreme Singing Heart," he said.

The book bird squawked and his box translated, "She who laid us has asked us to go into the world and find a new flock."

That was odd. I'd worked with Singing Heart when they set up the reservation. Alpha females never let go of their sons until they could find another female to take them in. Things had to be bad on the Rez for her to cut them loose.

"Where do you sleep?"

The book bird's box said, "At the church."

"Except on bingo night, knitter's club night, and days with AA meetings."

"Then we sleep in the park."

"But that's more difficult now. They cut down the bushes to keep the homeless out."

These two were definitely nest-mates.

The phone rang and Paul yelled, "It's Mrs. Topher. She wants to know where you are."

"Listen, I've got to go. Good luck in finding new flock members." I shut the door before the bird people could object.

I dumped *The Watch Perch* into the electronics recycle bin and changed from my mommy clothes—puke-stained shirt and yoga pants—to my work clothes of white shirt and blue pants. My resemblance to the male drones was not lost on me. I grabbed a not too stinky towel from the clothes hamper and nestled the hot pan of brownies on the front floorboards of the van. After fetching Cissie and buckling her into the child seat, Paul strolled out with my purse and Tyler.

He asked, "Aren't you going to take him with you?"

I tucked my purse behind my seat. "Did you clean out and refill the diaper bag like you promised?"

He made a Homer Simpson d'oh face.

I smiled sweetly. "Then, there's your answer."

As I backed out of the driveway, Paul came running from the front door, waving the plastic paper. I powered down the window.

"Take this with you. It keeps crawling out of the recycle bin. It beeps and says you owe at least a five-dollar donation."

Making a face, I took the paper. "I'll drop it off at the church on the way back." I shoved it under the brownies. They were no longer hot enough to melt it. Too bad.

Mrs. Topher was a sturdy woman with a toad-like mouth: thin-lipped and broad. This week her hair was an auburn color on the orange side. She lived on the biggest property with a pool deck the size of our entire house. I would've thought a competent stylist was within her budget.

Cissie joined the other kids playing tag outside the HOA's clubhouse, and I settled in the folding chair next to Mrs. Topher. As I cut and bagged the brownies, she added the label and the price.

"Are these boxed or homemade?"

"I baked them myself."

She marked them two for a dollar and tossed them in the boxed section. "Because you were forty-five minutes late, I assume you'll work the table until 12:45?"

It wasn't a question, but I didn't mind. There were activities for Cissie, and Mrs. Topher pounced on any poor victim who wandered within ten feet of the table, giving me time to wade through the impact statement. An hour in, Mrs. Topher became agitated after receiving a series of texts and calls.

I tried to ignore her harrumphing and heavy sighs, but it was a losing battle. "You seem upset, Mrs. Topher. Is there anything—"

"The cretin bailed on us."

I could see Mr. Topher in a cluster of men near the parking lot. So it wasn't a marital issue.

"This is the third investor. Third! They say they're interested, but once they see the engineer's report, they lose my phone number."

Now I understood. The HOA had been trying to get an investor to take over and finish up the subdivision. The bake sale was to help with attorney's fees. The original builder had gone belly up when he discovered it was harder to drain a swamp than he'd imagined.

"This idiot is suggesting we donate the land to the state as a designated wetlands."

"That would take care of—"

Her penciled-in eyebrows arched. "*If* you'd attended the last meeting, you'd *know* that the tax write-off will not offset the loss in fees. We'll have to raise the rates again. If there were only some way we could squash that stupid report."

"Cuz that wouldn't be illegal or anything," I said.

Mrs. Topher stared daggers at me.

~

By 1:15, Cissie and I were at the church. Vernon P. Hogg himself was setting up chairs for the 2 PM book club. Vern looked forty, despite being much younger. From his teeth, I suspected his drug of choice had been meth.

I handed him the plastic paper. "If this thing finds its way back to my house, I'll report you for littering."

He sighed and punched in a code. He dropped it in a pile on an old piano with chipped keys. It calmly sat there no longer flashing or inching toward me like a possessed credit card bill.

"Let's talk about the two bird people," I said.

"No, let's not. I was just trying to help them out, and all they've brought me is trouble." He opened a side door and yelled, "Hey, Larry and Curly! Get your feathered asses in here."

Cissie hid behind me, staring at the scary man. I folded my arms. "If they're Larry and Curly, who are you? Moe or Shemp?"

"Very funny. I didn't pick the names, they did."

The two bedraggled bird people hustled in, bowing and bobbing their long necks. In unison, they clicked an icon on their boxes. "How may we serve you, Father Hogg?"

I raised an eyebrow. Vernon said quickly, "I tol' you boys. You're supposed to say, 'How may we serve *Jesus*, Father Hogg?'"

The two bird people looked confused and corrected the text associated with that icon.

"It doesn't matter." He waved his fingers as if to shoo chickens. "You two are fired. Get out of my church and go darken someone else's doorstep." He turned to me. "Are you happy now?"

The two bird people screeched and flapped their clipped wings. "What have we done wrong? How can we make amends?"

They kept tapping the icons repeating those two sentences until Vernon grabbed a mop handle and threatened to beat them. Cissie burst into tears and threw herself in front of the bird people. Her little arms out wide, she yelled, "I won't let you hurt them!"

Cissie's action shocked Vernon. He sighed. "I told you all they do is get me in trouble."

I rested my hand on Cissie's head. She melted into my leg, wiping snot and tears on the back of her hand. The bird people clustered behind me and froze, as if that made them invisible.

"Jesus!" Vernon shouted. One of them had dumped his cloaca. "Look what I have to clean up!" He spun around twice on the broken-down heel of his faux alligator boots. "I got people comin'! Payin' people!"

Good thing *he* didn't have a cloaca.

"I don't want them fired," I said. "I just don't want anyone to take advantage of them."

"Taking advantage, hell. I'm helping *them* out!"

I pointed to the pile of *The Watch Perch*. I would've waved one in his face, but I feared touching them.

He whined, "I paid their vagrancy tickets for sleeping in the park."

Hands on hips, I asked, "Did you clip their wings?"

He shook his head. "They have to be clipped to get off the Rez. Some new regulation 'cuz people claimed they were peeking in windows and messing with security."

I'd heard about no-fly zones, but I hadn't thought through all the implications. "Can you keep them for a couple more days while I figure something out?"

"Not those two. They're dumber than pigeons. I'll keep the other three."

"Five? You're housing five bird people?"

"There're a dozen under the bridges near the river. They're pouring off the Rez, and they're all looking as sad as these two. I think they're starving."

I looked at my phone. If I ignored the speed limit, I could get to Singing Heart's compound in two hours. I called to Cissie, "Sweetheart, help the bird people into the van."

Cissie's entire being lit up. "I knew you would save them, mommy. I knew you would!" She herded them like ducks outside. I felt a flicker of pride before reality hit. I hadn't saved anyone.

~

Larry and Curly strutted through the backyard, eating insects, while I told Paul what happened. He squatted to Cissie's level. "Did you really do that? Protect those bird people?" She nodded fiercely. He gave her a bear hug. "I'm so proud of you."

My heart swelled. I kissed Paul on his neck. "You're a good man."

Cissie ran off to tell her dollies about her adventures. I fetched the car keys.

Paul shook his head. "It's late."

"I've got to see for myself. Something's up."

He looped his arm around my neck. "Sweetie, you can't save the world."

"No, but I simply walked away, and that's not working for me either." The emotion made my voice crack.

"You were burned out. With the commute and Tyler—"

"Yeah, but if I don't do anything at all, then I'm part of the problem. I don't want that to be the lesson I teach Cissie."

He met my eye. "After what Cissie did today, are you seriously worried?"

I smiled but hung my head. Paul got out his wallet and handed me cash.

"What's this for?"

"Gas. But I'm keeping the rest 'cuz I'm not making dinner. I'm ordering pizza."

~

I entered Reservation land at 4:40. It bordered the river in a swampy valley that produced mostly mosquitoes. Singing Heart's high status had afforded her first choice in picking her home nest site. It was the closest to the blacktop. The climate was hot and humid, but the birds liked it that way. I kept my windows up and the AC on. Singing Heart's people on average looked better than the two drones, but there were no children in the crèche and even the females were out in the river working.

The two male guards at the entrance of Singing Heart's aviary were still resplendent with long tails, elegant wings, and piercing black eyes. They sported the sharpened beak spikes and leg spurs of their class. One recognized me and asked me to wait. He sent a small messenger male inside. After a few minutes, I was ushered into the geodesic dome that functioned as Singing Heart's main dormitory.

Inside resembled a rain forest arboretum. Industrial fans created a slight breeze and made it easier for me to breathe. I walked slowly to keep from sweating too much. Designed for visitors and fledglings, the path wound upward. The adults glided from perches set along the struts two-thirds of the way up the sides. The top of the curved path opened onto a platform for meetings. Above that sat Singing Heart's nest. One of her daughters roosted in it. The other nests lay empty.

Singing Heart's frill was up and her feathers fluffed. On the platform, her brown and green plumage shone brightly in the late afternoon sun, but in the dappled places among the plants, she'd have blended in perfectly. Her neck extended, she stood tall. My eye met her beak. For the first time in her presence, I felt the flutter of discomfort and fear, as if the trouble—whatever it may be—was somehow my fault. I asked, "Did you release two males?"

Singing Heart's wings came away from her body, and all the other birds in the dome came to attention. "Yes. Why?"

Out of nowhere one of the male guards landed with a thump next to me.

I put my hand out in a placating motion. "They're at my house."

Singing Heart lifted her knees one at a time and shook out her feathers. The other birds relaxed, and the guard bird moved to the edge of the platform but did not fly off.

"They are good men, but we have no room for them."

"May I ask why?"

"Come. Walk with me."

Singing Heart could've glided to the exit in a heartbeat, but she walked slowly, one long stride after another, so I could keep up.

Once outside of the dome, Singing Heart flicked her tail feathers. The guard remained behind.

"Children can be impetuous and impatient," she said.

"Are you talking about these two males?" I asked.

"No. My eldest daughter. She couldn't control herself and fertilized two eggs. I'm sure you saw her nesting."

"Are resources so tight that you don't have room for two more?"

"It's a matter of leadership. If my home nest doesn't control its population, I can't ask that of others."

"The valley looks lush, is there a shortage of food?"

"Your government insists that unless we put in a water treatment plant, we can have no population growth. They say we're putting too much nitrogen into the water, but they won't allow us to sell our technology, or use it to back a security you call municipal bonds."

I pretended to examine the foliage to hide my chagrin. Singing Heart could read facial expressions, and her sight was superior to humans. Like most avians, she had an extra protein in the back of her eye and could see into the ultraviolet range. Her home star was very active and produced a lot of UV. In fact, it had become so active, it was eroding their planet's atmosphere. That's why they'd come to Earth, refugees from a natural disaster.

It *was* my fault. The clean water non-profit I worked for had been responsible for some of those clean water laws. *Talk about unintended consequences.* Now I understood why the state hadn't fought the legislation. It was never about clean water. It was about population control. The non-profit and I had been suckered.

"How about making a home nest in town where there are sewers?" I asked.

"None of my daughters can get building permits."

My own damn HOA had contributed to that problem.

We continued to the river. The water was clean but the banks boggy. Singing Heart waded out into the dark mud. She stretched her neck. It ballooned and she made a whooping roar that ended in a bellowing meow. All the females stopped what they were doing and responded. She called and they repeated for several rounds. The tone and pattern changed but not the volume. From downstream came a second set of calls and responses. When it did,

Singing Heart shook her feathers and rejoined me on hard ground. The call would wind its way down the river to the end of the valley.

I didn't need the translator. It was a gratitude psalm. A tear dripped down my cheek.

"Magdalene? What distresses you?"

My chin quivered. "How can you sing of gratitude considering how we treat you?"

"You've taken in my two sons. You cannot imagine my relief."

It had been a sheer accident. And for how long could I keep them? An aspirin for a brain tumor.

Singing Heart asked, "You left the AAB because you were having difficulties with a fledgling? Is he well?"

"I left because it was too much stress to deal with a toddler, a nursing infant, a sexist boss, and an hour commute each way." I blushed, ashamed of my pitiful problems. "I can't imagine how you handle the stress of this place."

Singing Heart bobbed her head. "I don't do it alone. I have my flock. Your culture of complete independence is foolish." She clucked and the box intoned, "You will do better now that you have my two sons. We have more to teach you than technology."

"Technology!" I pointed to the birds in the river. "Your daughters all have equivalents of Ph.D.s, and they are reduced to stringing nets in a river."

"Do you feel reduced when you take care of your fledglings?"

I remained silent. There were seasons in life, but my boss and my culture didn't understand that, so I did feel less than no matter how wrong it was. I lifted my chin. "I make no promises, but now that I understand the issues, I can work on solutions."

Singing Heart brushed me with a wing a sign of gratitude. But in this case, I took it as a gesture of forgiveness.

~

On Monday, instead of summarizing that 270-page impact statement, I presented the plight of the bird people. The staff members were divided as to what to do, but they agreed to an emergency board meeting to discuss the possible realignment of the mission of the non-profit. We were small and disorganized, but it was a start.

Moving on to the second prong of my master plan, I cornered Kendra—our one and only lawyer—before she could slip away to pick up her kids from school.

I handed her a flash drive with the HOA covenant rules. "My question is simple. Can I force the HOA to accept an application to build an aviary?"

"You *are* taking this personally," said Kendra.

"I want to change the narrative from NIMBY to YIMBY."

"YIMBY?"

"*Yes*, In My Back Yard."

Kendra smiled. "I'll go over this tonight and get back to you."

~

A week later, I was sitting in Mrs. Topher's living room with the finished proposal. Mrs. Topher's décor was 1970s day-glo. It explained the clown hair. I wanted to get down to business, but Mrs. Topher wanted to play hostess. She provided fat-free, taste-free cookies and iced tea so sweetened the sugar had precipitated into the bottom of the glass. My fillings ached.

"I hear there are two avians living in your home," said Mrs. Topher.

I'd read the rules so many times I knew that unrelated folk were frowned upon, but not live-in help. I smiled. "They provide childcare and cleaning services."

I expected Mrs. Topher to warn me of the dangers of salmonella or something, but instead she nodded slyly. "Yes, I've heard the labor laws don't apply. You don't have to pay unemployment or match social security." She patted me on the knee. "How smart of you. It must be nice to finally be able to afford help."

Ripping off Mrs. Topher's arm and beating her to death with it would not advance my agenda. Instead, I asked, "So you have no issues with bird people?"

"Not if they have a job, know their place. Of course not. I'm not a racist."

"Excellent. I have a buyer for the rest of the subdivision."

Mrs. Topher lit up, and not just from her spray tan.

I explained the details of how Singing Heart's daughter would buy into the subdivision and build an aviary. "And here's the best part, because they'll be part of the community, they'll pay yearly fees. It's a win-win."

Mrs. Topher's face darkened like a summer thunderstorm. "It won't pass."

"Why not?"

"I'll vote against it. This is a *human* community."

My time at the non-profit taught me not to argue. I'd just have to go grassroots.

Mrs. Topher opened a leather slipcase and produced a typed list. "I'll save you time. These people will vote with me no matter what. I engender loyalty that way."

Was she bluffing? I reminded myself not to engage. I thanked her for the list and tried to let myself out, but Hercules and Atlas were loose. I had to wait until Mr. Topher corralled the two guard dogs. They were well muscled, but a little too lean. I wondered if they were actually vicious or just hungry.

~

After dinner, I made some phone calls. Mrs. Topher hadn't bluffed. She had a solid thirty-five percent. The vote would fail. I wailed in frustration and flopped facedown into all the maps and papers I'd spread out on the table. Larry tapped the floor with one foot. I rested my chin in my hand. "Need help getting Cissie to bed?"

He typed on his controller, and the box said, "You are distressed. It is our role as men of the house to relieve that distress. How may we help?"

Just being asked made me smile. I hadn't explained about the proposal to shield them from disappointment, but the worst had come to pass so there was no point in hiding it. I explained the situation. While doing so, Curly joined us with Cissie padding right behind, her Disney toothbrush in hand.

I pointed on the map. "The woman who lives here will vote against the proposal, and all the people on this list," I held up the paper, "will vote with her."

Larry touched my shoulder with a beak, a very personal gesture. "Then all is not lost. All you have to do is change one person's mind instead of thirty. We have faith in you."

"Of course we do, mommy." Cissie hugged me.

Yeah. Only one.

~

After the kids were in bed and the bird people asleep, I gathered the covenant rules and binder clipped them. I found a loose page under the map of the subdivision. It outlined the rules governing utility easements. Something caught my eye. I compared the Google satellite view with the subdivision map. The original map didn't have Mrs. Topher's giant pool and deck. I checked the property lines, the easements, and compared it to the satellite view.

"Son of a—" I fished out two steaks from the deep freezer and shoved them into the microwave to defrost.

Twenty minutes later, dressed all in black with a measuring tape in one hand and a bag 'o steaks in the other, I stood at the Tophers' fence. Hercules and Atlas barreled up barking and snarling.

"Hey, boys." I waved the steaks. "Let's find out. Are you vicious or hungry?"

~

The next day I again sat in Mrs. Topher's living room, suffering another glass of sludge tea.

She smiled unctuously. "You said you needed a change to the agenda?"

I'd used that as the excuse. There was no way this woman would forfeit an opportunity to gloat. "Yes."

"Do you want to cancel the vote?"

"No. I have discovered a violation." I leaned in. "A serious violation. The board needs to know so they can act."

Mrs. Topher licked her lips. "Do tell."

I handed her a manila folder. Eagerly, she flipped it open. She scowled. "This is my address."

I grinned. "Yes, and your pool crosses into the easement by nine inches. You'll have to rip it out."

"I'll get a variance."

"That'll take 2/3rds too. Do you think you'll have that many friends after they find out you could've solved both the swamp problem and reduced their fees by allowing the aviary?"

She tossed the folder onto the coffee table. "That's blackmail."

"May I count on your vote and those of your friends?"

As I rounded the van to the driver's side, Mrs. Topher released Hercules and Atlas. They bolted straight for me, but instead of mauling me, they tried to lick me to death. Disgusted, Mrs. Topher slammed her front door. *Such bad doggies.*

~

Two months later, the subdivision threw a party for the groundbreaking. Larry and Curly's flight feathers had filled in and their tails were elongating. Their crests stood high and their eyes shone. By Christmas, they might be ready for their own set of leg spurs.

They followed Tyler, as he stumbled across the lawn. He'd grown into a mobile terror, squealing and clapping his hands. Seeing the three of them walk across the lawn, my heart warmed. Flocks were nice.

The ceremony had called all the displaced birds from miles around. They would all apply to become a part of the newest home nest. All but Larry and Curly, of course. First, she was their sister, and second, they'd become fully integrated into our household. I had become their mother bird.

Paul strolled over with Cissie on his shoulders. Behind them stood Mrs. Topher, her hair now a yellow-orange. She preened for a local news team. "Yes. We are a progressive neighborhood. *I* was instrumental in getting the permits."

Paul nodded towards Larry and Curly. "Boy howdy, are those two working out, especially now that you're back at the AAB."

"Don't get too used to it," I said. "Soon, we might not be able to afford them."

Paul frowned. "Why?"

"My next project is to get the bird people labor protections."

Cissie said in her father's ear, "Yes, daddy. Do you know what labor protections are?"

As he bee-lined to the food table, he said, "Yes, I do, Cissie. But please explain them to me anyway."

My attention turned to three clipped birds in white button-downs and khakis who rushed toward Larry, Curly, and Tyler. The leader of the three clutched a black book. The other two clutched

MAD SCIENTIST JOURNAL: AUTUMN 2019

plastic papers, which flickered with text.

The leader squawked and the box translated, "Good day, gentle birds. We are seeking to increase our flock. Have you been saved by Jesus?"

Larry and Curly stood tall, their necks extended. In unison, they said, "Thank you, but we have already been saved, saved by Mary Magdalene."

––––––––

Ms. Mary Magdalene Farconi, a working mother, is a G-11 in the Labor Protections Department of the Alien Affairs Bureau. She supervises a governmental hotline for reporting labor abuse of Avian Nationals and is currently working with cities all over the US to design and develop aviaries within human communities.

––––––––

Dr. Kathy Kitts, a former geology professor, served as a science team member on the NASA Genesis Discovery Mission. Before that, she directed a planetarium for nine years. Her latest speculative short fiction has appeared in *Amazing*, *James Gunn's Ad Astra*, and *Mad Scientist Journal*. Her latest short story collection, *Getting What You Need*, is now available on Amazon. Born and raised in the southwest, she is currently living in the high desert of New Mexico.

A LEAGUE OF HER OWN

An essay by Beth Cantrell, as provided by Robert Dawson

I've gone into space with some odd ducks, but let me tell you, Loreena Saunders was one of the oddest.

On those early missions to Mars, you got five fricking kilos for personal effects. A few pieces of jewellery, perhaps a favorite silk scarf, and a thumbdrive or two. And maybe some photographs and a lock of hair, if you weren't smart enough to leave old memories behind.

Some people brought musical instruments. A couple people had pennywhistles, and there were a few lightweight electric violins and guitars, little more than fingerboard, strings, and pickup. "Mac" Duncan even had an electronic bagpipe, about the size of a big soda straw. Better yet, he had earbuds for practice.

But what sort of nut would take a baseball and a first baseman's mitt to Mars—a third of an astronomical unit away from the nearest baseball diamond, even at conjunction? Loreena, that's who. Back when she was a kid in Boston, she'd played Little League with the boys, and she'd been on the varsity women's team at MIT. Here, she couldn't even go outside and play catch: the glove wouldn't fit over her p-suit. But if she minded, it didn't show: when she had nothing else to do, she'd sit around the dome, slapping the ball into the glove, smiling blissfully, and occasionally picking an imaginary pop fly out of the air. The constant slap of leather on leather could get on your nerves.

So when I got sent up to Phobos to do the preliminary geological survey (I'll go with "areological" for Mars, but "phobological" just sounds silly), my excitement was damped when I realized that Loreena was going to be my assistant. The orbiter we were going in was about the size of the minivan my folks had when I was a kid. The galley was a cupboard full of freeze-dried food in single-serving pouches and a gadget for injecting warm water into them. It had two tiny berths, with privacy doors so thin you could hear somebody breathe through them. I wondered if I could get somebody else, but Loreena was the only colonist with geological training who could also pilot the orbiter. I was stuck with her.

"You're not going to bring that baseball of yours, are you?" I asked.

She grinned. "You're bringing your Rubik's Cube, aren't you, Beth?"

I clenched my teeth. When I was twenty, I'd been the CalTech women's champion, and in fifth place nationally for the "five peeks" event. I wasn't quite that fast anymore, but old cubists never die, they just lose face. Of course I was bringing my cube. "I'll try to keep it quiet," I said.

"Don't worry, probably neither of us will have time to actually use them. Have you seen the task schedule?"

Dammit, she was right. The schedule called for us to spend twelve hours per sol taking rock and soil samples, or measuring magnetism, radioactivity, and gravitational anomalies. After that, they estimated an hour for filing reports and another for habitat maintenance. A sol's longer than a day, but only by thirty-seven minutes. There wasn't going to be any slack time.

Just before departure, we were stowing our personal gear in the orbiter. Loreena pointed at a tell-tale right-angled corner pushing out the thin fabric of my tote bag. "Ha!" she said. "Caught in the act, Beth!"

"And I suppose you're going to tell me you don't have a baseball and glove in there?" I said, pointing at her bag.

"Why would I bring a baseball and glove to Phobos?" she asked, innocently. "Is there a pickup game scheduled or something?"

And that was all I could get out of her. I wondered if I could sneak my cube back into the dome complex, but it was too late.

~

The first thing you notice about Phobos is the gravity, one two-thousandth of a gee. Or, rather, you don't notice it; it's like free-fall

76

MAD SCIENTIST JOURNAL: AUTUMN 2019

with a very slight drift. It takes you about a minute to fall a meter; if you jumped off a kilometer-high cliff and didn't die of boredom on the way down, you could land on your feet, unhurt. If the orbiter hadn't had screw pitons to lock its legs down to the ochre regolith, Loreena and I could have lifted it up between us and carried it away. Jumping over it was easier than going around it.

On the first sol, we were out on the surface, working our way up towards the ridge on the edge of Stickney Crater that's the high point of Phobos. Mars hung overhead, a huge orange beachball just out of reach. We carried fifty kilos of apparatus each, and still weighed next to nothing. Our eyes told us that were climbing towards a huge dome—Phobos is shaped like a lumpy baking potato—but it felt like spacewalking. We wore crampons with blunt five-centimeter spikes, but even so, we had no more purchase for our feet in the loose regolith than if we'd been on ice. We moved by slow careful hops, trying not to lose control or to slow ourselves down by going too high. In each hand we carried meter-long pieces of thick-walled aluminum tube with improvised wrist straps: sometimes we used them like ski poles to push against the ground, and mid-jump we used their mass to balance ourselves, like tightrope walkers.

For maybe the fifth time, we stopped to make our measurements. Once we were done, I began to lift the gravimeter onto my back—awkwardly, it was the size of a refrigerator and had every gram of that mass. Just then, Loreena tried to bend down. Her legs drifted upward, of course, and I laughed as she paddled her arms in circles to rotate herself. She began to somersault forward, and after a few seconds, was able to pick up the thing she'd seen. A light-colored rock, round, about the size of an orange. She reversed the paddling until she got her feet back under her, then she looked at the rock appraisingly, and plopped it into her sample pouch without explanation. She shouldered the gamma ray spectrometer, and we floated on upward.

When we got to the top of the ridge, Loreena put down her gear, hefted the rock, and grinned at me. I looked at the way she was holding it. Not an orange, I thought. A baseball.

"Watch this!" she said. Then she wound up and pitched it in the general direction of the flattened north pole, about fifteen klicks away. It was a lazy creampuff of a pitch, but pretty damn good for somebody in a p-suit. She regained her balance and watched as it drifted away. "Hope I got the speed right," she said.

"Right for what?"

"Beth, you've just witnessed the birth of Phobos's moon. Which I hereby name 'Rivera.'"

"Rivera? You mean the Mexican painter?"

"*Mariano* Rivera," she said. "He pitched for the Yankees. Back at the beginning of the century."

Of course.

For the next few weeks, Loreena tracked that rock obsessively. She set the lander's telescopes to look for it every time it passed overhead. Because she'd used the highest point of Phobos for a pitcher's mound, Rivera was too far above the lander to see with the naked eye, but our fifty-centimeter reflector could spot it easily. It passed over a different region every time, as Phobos spun beneath it, so sightings were irregular, but the computer kept watch twenty-four-point-mumble hours per sol. When Loreena made the computer display the orbit, it looked like a messy ball of string. And I mean messy—with that crazy shape, Phobos is all gravitational anomalies.

At first it was hit-or-miss, but the more data she gathered, the more accurate her predictions got, and eventually she'd pull me over to the monitor just in time to see Rivera pass overhead. Even better, it got to the point where little deviations could be measured and used to determine those local variations in gravity. After a while we were getting almost as much data about mascons from that rock of Loreena's as we were from the million-dollar gravimeter. We wrote a paper about that technique; prospectors use it on asteroids now.

With only two sols left to go before our return date, I woke to Loreena pounding on the thin plastic hatch that was the door of my berth. "Hey! Beth! Get dressed! Rivera's gonna pass low over the ridge next orbit!"

I was tempted to tell her to go to hell, but I turned my berth light on and struggled into my tights and p-suit. We went out onto the surface, and headed up the ridge, drifting over the powdery regolith in long bounds. Neither of us had anything along but our walking poles. Without our usual burdens, and with the benefit of three weeks' experience of Phobian microgravity, we made easy progress.

"What are we doing?" I asked after a few minutes, uncomfortably aware that in my half-awake state I hadn't cleared this with Mars.

"You'll see, Beth. You'll see."

We sailed up toward Stickney for another few minutes, while I gradually grew more annoyed. "Dammit, Loreena, I'm in charge here, remember?" I said. "I need to know what's going on."

"Well, we've finished our gravimetric mapping of Phobos, right?"

Thanks to all that extra data from Rivera, we'd completed that part of the mission early. "Yes," I said. "But what are we doing now?"

We were at the top of the ridge. Loreena turned to me. "You'll find out in three minutes," she said, like a little girl planning a surprise for her mom. She waited, quietly; I was too tired to argue. "One minute." She laid one of her walking poles carefully on the ground, grasped one end of the other in both hands, and took a familiar stance.

"You're not—"

"Oh, yeah? Watch me!"

There it was, a tiny white dot in the brilliant sunlight, drifting towards us. Loreena lined herself up, whooped, swung, and knocked it in a high trajectory, right out of the ballpark. Right out of Phobos' gravity well, too—the scope never spotted it again. She regained her balance, put down her improvised bat, grinned, and raised her hand for a high five.

I couldn't help myself: I began to laugh. "Nice hit, Loreena!" I said. "But why not leave Rivera as a moon?"

"He pitched for the Yankees, remembah? And I'm from Bawston." She exaggerated her accent, as if to prove her claim.

"So?"

"Well, Beth, where I come from, we root for the Red Sox—and whoever beats the Yankees."

See what I mean? In a league of her own.

Beth Cantrell is best known for her award-winning paper "Simplified Passive Satellite Gravimetry" with L. Saunders. She holds the Mars, Phobos, Ceres, Vesta, and Pallas records for solving a Rubik's Cube in a p-suit. She sometimes goes to baseball games, but only if somebody promises to supply her with sufficient peanuts and Cracker Jack.

———————————

Robert Dawson teaches mathematics at a Nova Scotian university. He has had more than seventy SF stories published in periodicals ranging from *Nature* to *Mad Scientist Journal*. He'd like to congratulate MSJ on a great run, and thinks the plan to commemorate the last issue by blowing up the Sun is a very appropriate tribute to the close of an era.

IN COMMUNION WITH THE INVISIBLE FLOCK: ERASMUS KARL AND THE NIDIFICANT MANUSCRIPT

An essay by Luisa Sontag, as provided by George Salis

"If thy heart were a nest, thou would begat many birds."
—*The Purloined Philosophia* by Boris of Aventaria

There has been much controversy, even mythology, surrounding the so-called "nidificant manuscript." A few notables, including the biolinguist Norman Mast, have clamored to call it "an anachronistic masterpiece of scientific literature" (34), suggesting it has been passed down to us from the future, or an alternate past. Many others have deemed the work "a hoax of adolescent caliber" (Mare 25). But by studying the work and delineating its influence on human society, we can say that the truth exists somewhere between fantastic worship and ignorant dismissal. First of all, we know that this some 1,600-page manuscript was composed in the early 19th century by the naturalist, or "supernaturalist," Erasmus Karl, and details the existence of a species of bird-human that inhabits an archipelago called the Beak-born Islands. A number of its pages include baroque maps of the islands in question, along with illustrations of alien flora and fauna and, most importantly and prominently, the winged beings themselves.

This year marks the 150th anniversary since the first bottle, containing a page of Karl's manuscript, was discovered, specifically between the pincers of a bleached crab on the coast of Budva, Montenegro. This, the method in which Karl "published" the manuscript, has only added to the idiosyncrasy that has either converted or disgusted relevant experts. Each and every page was rolled into its own bottle and cast into the sea. During the intervening century and a half, around a dozen bottles washed ashore on all countries with a seaside (their contents now published *en masse* for the first time). The bottles were molded with aid of fire from a translucent shell later identified in the manuscript as a "Clay Conch, a most copious & convenient Resource of Nature." Ascertaining the location of the archipelago based on the appearance of the bottles has proved to be impossible, and the results obtained by oceanographers inexplicably suggest that the islands are capable of nautical mobility, like a flock, perhaps with occasional murmurations. Because bottled pages are still being discovered almost every month, the nidificant manuscript is most definitely incomplete, its prospective length up for debate. Some have purported that an infinite number of bottles will find their way to land, that they will continue to do so far after human civilization is but dust.

~

The Wind Calleth: A Brief Biography of Erasmus Karl

Before I begin my exploration of the manuscript and its influence on human society, I find it necessary to relate what is known of Erasmus Karl's life. Born in the Netherlands circa 1770, his mother was appalled at newborn baby Karl's full head of white feathery hair, his thin, elongated body, and the downy web between his taloned fingertips. She blamed the sins of the unknown father, while others whispered that Karl's appearance was the byproduct of a professionally prurient mother. Regardless of their origin, the unfortunate mutations condemned Karl as an outcast, something to be shooed, ogled, or at best tolerated. It wasn't long until young Karl despised his reflection, taking extreme measures to change it, as is written in his unpublished journals. First he shorn his hair, which highlighted his teardrop-shaped skull, then he filed his fingernails, sometimes with such desperation that he exposed and bloodied the nail beds, and finally he searched for a type of glove that could hide the finger webbings. Deeming the search futile, he excised the vein-thin skin as if it were the film on a Dutch custard. He bled profusely the first time, but afterward it was merely a matter of maintaining the V-shaped scabs.

Aside from his repelling physical characteristics, Karl was a relatively normal and healthy young boy, until, later in school, he became obsessed with nests, spurred by one he had witnessed being constructed outside his bedroom window. He was amazed to see it built with not just twigs and leaves, but clothespins, apple slices, strands of a stranger's hair, the string from a cup-and-ball, and other miscellaneous objects. The peculiarity of it inspired him to craft his own nests, which he planted, waiting for random birds to make them home. Impatient, he began to track down authentic nests in trees and the nooks of buildings and replace them with his synthetic ones. Some of his nests resembled the real thing, while others were of odd shapes, pyramids and Klein bottles, or made from strange materials, such as quasicrystals and gaseous gelatins. He was compelled to record the birds' reactions to their new homes. Some of them simply moved elsewhere, while others were driven to infanticide, either eating their younglings or dashing their unhatched shells against rocks. He was further horrified to discover that sphere-shaped nests of chlorophyll caused the birds' wings to deteriorate into stubs but was later pleased to determine that alabaster dodecahedrons produced birds with wingspans up to five feet. Other nests also seemed to have a positive effect, causing the inhabitants to sing more beautifully, to love their chirping chicks more so than ever before.

Being neglected by his mother, and without a father, the young Karl couldn't help but wonder why humans didn't live in similar nests of compassion, and through some such lines of logic he extrapolated that certain humans do live in those nests, bird-humans that exist in isolation from the rest of the world, on top of a mountain higher than Olympus, or on an island better concealed than Atlantis. Thereafter, he dedicated his time to further study of all birds while simultaneously looking for clues as to the whereabouts of the theoretical bird-humans, whom he soon thought of as his vanished ancestors.

Hence the term "nidificant manuscript," the adjective coming from the Latin *nīdificāre*, meaning "to nest" or "to build a nest," the impetus of his life's work. There is an irony here, in which the curse is also the gift, or vice versa. This is embodied most of all in events that occurred in the final years of Karl's formal education. Bullying became a constant impediment to Karl's mental stability. When required to change into athletic wear, the other boys gagged at Karl's mangled hands, smacked him on his goose-pimpled scalp, and poked him between his peninsular ribs. They spread rumors, asserting that his mother never carried him in her belly, but incubated a yellow-spotted egg for nine months, after having performed coitus with a chicken. Enveloped in that negative atmosphere, an incident brewed. Some said Karl wanted to defy the rumors, transcend them, while others said he wanted to reinforce them, integrate them as a form of truth. Whatever his beliefs or intentions at the time, he found himself standing at the edge of the school building's roof and, after yelling something, he jumped off, falling two stories as he flapped his phalanges. The webbing between his fingers had been regrown, which suggests experiment on Karl's part, yet a few witnesses reported that he was thrown off by a group of bullies and had no desire to fly. After being carried on a stretcher to the hospital, he was diagnosed with a broken hip and a slight fracture of the femur. During his bedridden months following an operation, he would repeat the following phrase, sometimes in a slow whisper, other times so loudly and quickly it sounded less like words and more like squawking: "The Wind calleth!" "The Wind calleth!" Such is also what he presumably shouted before his failed "experiment." One of the nurses claimed that when she put an ear to his bedroom door during those more boisterous moments of layered chanting, the birds outside his window squawked in response, initiating conversations that ceased the second she knocked.

It is thought that those cross-species conversations provided the first clues Karl needed to find the bird-humans (whom he subsequently labeled *Homo sapiens avis*: "wise bird man"). Not much is known of his life after he recovered from his fall. He did drop out of school in favor of more private research, and afterward his mother formally disowned him, wanting to distance herself as much as possible from his reputation for eccentric and anti-social behavior. He was rarely seen outside the wooden dome he built for himself at the edge of the forest. The few papers he attempted to publish in those early years are lost. We know only the title of one as it appeared in a letter of rejection: "The Nidus & the Fowl: Mutations of Mind & Body by way of Avian Architecture." A decade later, in 1801, Karl's "nest" was noticed as dilapidated by curious locals, who peered inside to find a mass of miasmic ingredients and piles of hastily scribbled notes, some of which might have contained proto-maps. Tucked in the walls of the nest as if part of the very structure were items pilfered or "recycled," such as human hair, newspapers, jewelry, and a pair of dirty women's underwear. There was no sign of Karl himself. Astounded and infuriated, the locals thought the nest a bastion of black magic and quickly burned it. They also assumed that the witchery had consumed the practitioner, that a cacodaemon snatched Karl from his bed at night. In truth, once Karl's preliminary research was completed, he left for the Beak-born Islands, an archipelago consisting of four large islands and some thirteen islets. Viewed from above, they vaguely form the shape of a bird's beak.

It is a mystery as to how Karl made it to the Beak-born Islands, though some allege that for part of his journey, he sailed with the crew of an unnamed British schooner, where he learned English. Whether true or not, it is generally believed that he never left the archipelago. As I will explain in detail later, the Beak-born Islands were his one true home, his "rapturous Nest" (47). Reinforcing the settlement theory, Karl became proficient in their immensely difficult language: "Subsequently bonding with these avian Beings as though I too were bless'd with Wings, I learn'd Their Language, a coalescence of shrill & protract'd Clicks, but with myriad Quavers & what can only be describ'd as Loops & Spirals, tallying a Complexity unheard of in any contemporary Language. Aye, One could only do these Beings Justness by chronicling Them in Their own sacr'd Tongue" (vi-vii). Which explains why some of the manuscript's pages include cryptographic ink marks consisting of curlicues, crests and troughs, and hypnotic helixes. Translators have yet to decipher them. But, as we will see, even though we can read a majority of the manuscript, it still births many more questions than it answers.

~

Begetting Many Birds: The Winged Beings and their Influence on Human Society

Some of the questions that the manuscript creates are due to the nature of history, others the nature of science. Yet most, perhaps, are the product of the nature of Nature. For example, it remains to be determined as to why, throughout the manuscript, we are given numerous descriptions and illustrations of the beings' wings, all of which contradict each other: "The foremost

Magnetism of Their pseudo-primitive Rituals were indubitably the arcing Wings, resplendent with feather'd Colors the like of which no Man has ever laid Eyes upon" (261), "& when They alight on the sheer Tips of Their two-digit'd Feet They fold Their iridescent, scaly Wings & seem well-nigh Human, for as cumbersome as the Appendages may appear, they are afford'd the Ability to retract into two large vertical sun-on-the-horizon-shap'd cavities in the Back, flanking the spik'd Spine" (333-334), "To my Dismay, some of Them Drown'd in the Waters betwixt Land—in what could only be christen'd as Rivulets in contrast to the mighty Ocean that enclos'd Them, isolat'd them from all Civilizations. Such Calamities were ow'd to the tuft-laden Nubs which were so infantile in Structure, though mature in their Growth. These superficially suppress'd Extremities only permitt'd Them to drift diminutive Distances, to fleetingly hover forward" (455-456), and "In Stretches of Jubilation They were beheld to fly as high as the Sun itself, encircl'd in the Incandescence, Their Wings the extent of a mythological Bird, fleck'd with fiery Eyes" (999).

In the context of these quotations, evolution is neither discussed nor acknowledged, and we are led to believe that every being possessed every type of wing, although not exactly simultaneously. One colleague of mine conjectured that time in this archipelago is not like we know it, that the experience of time is disjointed, perhaps utterly capricious. Even physicists are uncertain as to whether our Laws are universal in the ultimate meaning of the word. If this hypothesis of chaotic time is true, then Karl observed the evolution of wings in a relatively brief period but processed the gradualism as a stasis. This evolution must have been guided heavily by the development of their nests' structure, descriptions of which also suffer from contradiction: "Their Nests, which grac'd the tops of decapitat'd Trees, were hierarchical, bas'd upon the breadth & altitude of said Trees, with the Dimensions of the Throne Nest rivaling the almightiest Redwood" (200), "Evoking the Greek Phoenix, They slumber'd in domestic Groupings within grandiose Campfires, roosting upon the heat'd Coals in Symbiosis, for those Coals were the Backs of Combustible Crabs, who were also commission'd in Spells of Conflict" (606), and "Never had I beheld such gargantuan Leaves, affix'd to such slender Stalks. Sounder than Diamond, the wing'd Beings carv'd Spears from them. I was further mystifi'd when I hearken'd to how Winds, lac'd

86

with twilit Sea Salt, caus'd the bamboo Trunks to knell, soaping the Air with soporific if inhuman Mantras. More like Flies than Birds, They made Homes of the Leaves' Undersides, adhering with a viscous Substance that secret'd from both Palms & Soles" (1,122-1,123). For this reason, and others previously mentioned, chronology in the manuscript as a whole is defied. What the reader sees published is but one construction of many possibilities, a snapshot of the flock in flight, as it were.

Of course, another question is: Why did the bird-humans—if capable of flight, depending on the type of wing they possessed at a given time—remain only on the Beak-born Islands? Why did they not migrate to other lands, make contact with human civilization? According to Karl:

> Their Religion bequeath'd to Them the Knowledge that Nothing exist'd beyond Their Islands & Sprinkle of Islets. As such, They believ'd I arriv'd from either Above or Below. I was either Mole or Swallow. Devil or Angel, if you will. To divine my Color They subject'd me to a Trial. They serv'd me a Bowl of Their own gourmet Delicacy, White Worms, which I willingly ate out of Respect, & dare conclude their Flavor was akin to spic'd Raisins. Such a Worm, I later learn'd, is pestilential to the Mole Stomach. Afterward, They slic'd my Palm with a Clay Conch Blade, taking turns at tasting my Blood. They seem'd repuls'd at first, Their Owl Eyes flaring more so, Their Heads revolving 180 Degrees & back again, but it must have been the Rush of the Aftertaste that made Them Hoot with Hedonism. 'Uh-Uh-Above!' (8-9)

Aside from Karl, there is the possibility that contact between humans and the winged strangers occurred again, although much later, and in the unlikeliest of locales. One might say, in heaven. (An earlier and quite different encounter, one of both confrontation and conviviality, will be mentioned later.) To understand, we must learn more from Karl about their beliefs and intentions:

> As much as They play'd & pierc'd the Clouds from within, Their Kind had more than mere nubivagant Tendencies. Rather, They worshipp'd the Stars, longing to fly amongst them, to

fertilize the scintillating Surfaces like a Bee upon the Flower, for Their Conception of those distant Dots of Light was akin to an infinite Meadow in which the Center of Flowers coruscat'd o'er altitudinous Realms, and thus beckon'd, perchance even taunt'd, the Beings to Pinnacles anew. Legend had it, One of Their Populace did indeed sunder the Surface of the Sky & found Herself floating among the Stellar Flowers. Her Constellation, eponymously nam'd ¡Khoro[1], is delineat'd by Seven Stars, One of which is Man's Northern, thus She was subsum'd within that Meadow of the Cosmos. Other Acolytes were martyr'd but not beatifi'd in the same Manner. Flapping through the Spheres of the Sky, They would succumb to the Wintriness & fall back as icy Gargoyles, shattering upon an Island or buoying in the Sea 'til They liquefi'd into crystal-ridden Spume. Naturally, They mourn'd Their Dead & would orchestrate aerial Funerals, prancing & pirouetting at such a colossal Elevation that They resembl'd Motes in a Glass of Water. Using Clay Conches or other sundry Materials, grieving Mothers would jar a modest Portion of the Sea a Day after a frozen Martyr fell into it, Their equivalent of Ashes in an Urn. (78-79)

The winged beings' propensity for spacefaring might explain the "vision" astronaut J.P. Torring claimed to have witnessed while on the moon for Apollo 14. Ridiculed and disbelieved by friends, family, and most of the public, Torring explained what he saw in an interview, "I'd call it, you know, like one of those damned harpies. Something, you know ... something your parents might scare the bejesus out of you with to make you behave. A damned big closet monster with ... with tiger claws, chicken feet, you know, and wings made of alloy or something. It looked part machine as much as poultry. But with, oh gosh ... with a human face" (39). According to Torring, the bird-human stared him down with equal parts fear and curiosity, before beating its wings in a storm of moon dust and heading for the stars. Unfortunately, Torring's fellow astronauts did not corroborate his story. For a period after that infamous interview, people across the U.S. and some abroad claimed to have

---

[1] According to Karl, "The tospy-turv'd Exclamation Mark betokens a helical Whistle most conventional in the Bird-humans' Elocution of formal Addresses." (3)

been bound in their beds, gagged with silver powder, and sat on by chromium angels, although such claims of abduction or visitation are dismissed by skeptics as frauds and delusions. Amateur astronomers also interpreted at that time certain spectral data as vast fleets of them soaring between galaxies in the formation of a luminous arrowhead a thousand earths wide, but this scientific conclusion is controversial (Krasznahorkai 24-59).

Controversy seems inseparable from any notion of the bird-humans, however distant in relation or idea, as with their method of copulation. Karl explains that sexual intercourse was never a taboo in that isolated society. Rather, they indulged quite often in a variety of positions, many familiar, if not shunned or banned, by human civilization. Yet only a specific sexual act produced offspring, whereas the rest existed for pleasure's sake. In no sparse prose does Karl illuminate the bizarre act:

> Much like the Red-tail'd Hawk, They would Woo each Other by flying in Circles, Triangles, & Hexagons. The Male & Female both would dive steeply & rise steeply. O, Gloriousness! Then, when the Volition struck at the Center of Their Souls, They would hold feather'd Hands, entangle Talon'd Feet, & dive in a Blur of phantasmal Colors, pecking each Other's Cheeks & Beaks with love-saturat'd Smeerkins. But, O Foulness!, not all Unions end'd in unanimous Life. If, perchance, They become too enraptur'd in Rapture to perceive impending Ground, such Soul-dives on Occasion result'd in a bespatter'd Death for the Lovers. Yet, O Propitiousness!, an inseminat'd Egg would still hatch & rise as a human Phoenix, not from the Ashes, but from the Gore of the Hatchling's Progenitors, Born an Orphan. These strange & estrang'd Offspring, who possess'd a crimson Complexion, were treat'd as Lepers by the rest of Their Kith & Kin, forc'd to fend for Themselves or form minuscule Factions with a more savagely-inclin'd Temperament, enduring on the Edges of Islets. Contrariwise, a Child born from a Soul-dive which end'd with a Plunge in the Ocean would be a Child Born to different & deeper Doom. Though lungless at the Moment of Conception, come Accouchement its Lungs would be chock-full of Seawater. O, ill-fat'd! A Child born Drown'd. (171)

Somehow, this way of lovemaking has thrice seeped into human society in the form of controversy as much as tragedy. An obscure French filmmaker named Absolon Dubois, who begrudged and attempted to compete with Georges Méliès, can be credited with making one of the first pornographic films. Yet it wasn't his intention to be lewd. Rather, he thought the film a "testament to pure science," and based the premise on what he deemed, without elaboration, a "divine source material" (Oro 10). Titled *In the Sky of the Tesseractyles*, it was shown at the brink of a millennium in 1898 to an elite audience of intellectuals. The actors in the film, devoid of clothes, hang upside down by well-concealed wires. With a vertical scrolling sky of painted clouds in the background, the pairs thrust in and out of each other as a wind-machine from below blows their hair and wings about. Some of the pairs screech sweet nothings to their mates in the form of clicks and whoops that a linguist in the audience later called "ethereal Morse code, as mesmerizing as it is unintelligible" (18). Starting with cirrus and continuing through stratus, the green-brushed ground finally appears, but rather than creating nests of gore, a substitution splice allows the death-diving bird-humans to disappear in a plume of blue-stained smoke. The scene then transitions to a close-up of a golden egg branded with sacred geometry. A time-lapse of the hatching reveals a newborn baby boy with an albatross' beak for a mouth. There the film ends. Many praised the uncanny wings of the actors, which were made of glass and contained a representation of four dimensions or higher, a tesseract in wing form. One viewer, a distinguished physicist, said the "wings have more than a life of their own, they have the Cosmos in their curvature" (18). A paleontologist, who sat in the back and scrutinized the film with the aid of a monocle, was stuck on what he called the "terrible pterodactyl pun. These humanoid birds are anything but similar to my winged reptiles," although he later admitted that "the film has penetrated my dreams in ways that the bones of prehistoric monsters never could" (19). Almost a year later, Dubois was found dead in his home, any sign of foul play absent on his body, but with the incinerated work of a sequel four feet from his outstretched hand. Méliès was interrogated by the police but presented a viable alibi, leaving the circumstances of Dubois' death forever ambiguous, his cinematic potential snuffed.

Upon rediscovery, Absolon Dubois' *In the Sky of the Tesseractyles* was shown in 1930 on a week-long loop at a gallery of cinema in lower Manhattan. Perhaps inspired by the film, a rash of romantic suicide pacts occurred, wherein nude couples tipped themselves over a steel rib of the Empire State Building's embryonic skeleton, tumbling while linked at the loins. Later, the same style of self-slaughter transpired on September 11, 2001, in which co-working lovers undressed themselves, embraced each other, and dove from the tower into funnels of fire-flaked smoke, their intertwined bodies an expression of life and love against the presence of cult-inspired death. While writing this paper, a colleague brought to my attention a missing page of the *Kama Sutra*, recently discovered, that describes the "upside-down lovers, suspended in wind," whose sexual organs were secondary to the "tumescent wings of their hollow spines" (69). Love between souls, claims the text, is fully realized in this mystical position, during which "all else dissolves" (70).

Yet for all the influences from the society of bird-humans that I have noted, the most clandestine and far-reaching is found in Charles Darwin's seminal work. Readers might find the following quote familiar: "There is Grandeur in this Way of Life, with its avian Powers, having been originally breath'd into a few Forms or into One; & that, whilst this Planet has ignorantly gone cycling on according to the fix'd Laws that Man knows, from so simple & hidden a Beginning endless Wings most beautiful & most wonderful have been, & are being, Evolv'd" (1,631). This is the final paragraph of, not *On the Origin of Species*, but the published arrangement of Karl's manuscript (and the only time Karl mentions evolution, which suggests that he may have adapted to the islands' nature of chaotic time, in mind as well as body, a phenomenon described later). A paragraph which Darwin, were he still alive, would have to answer to. That is, if the similarity were to be taken at face value. Far from plagiarism, a different story is told in Karl's manuscript:

Due to the Essence of the Beak-born Islands, I am certain that if a Man had discover'd Them, he must in some Capacity be Pure of Mind & Heart. However, as in the Mythologies of bygone Civilizations, there exists Techniques to sneak into Utopia. Thus, when an Eagle-ey'd Sentinel station'd at One of the Wind Towers first spi'd the *Beagle* on the Skyline, He warn'd the Fowl Lord, who then command'd His Flock to assume the long-practic'd Formations, encloaking Themselves in Their chameleon Wings, proficiently camouflag'd with the Texture of Stones. While many masquerad'd Themselves as the inanimate Landscape, Others imbib'd shamanic Potions which shape-shift'd Them into Mockingbirds, Giant Tortoises, & most disgusting, clumsy Lizards. When the Man who identifi'd himself as Darwin came ashore, I was strangely unsurpris'd to find that he resembl'd me, minus the avian Mutations that I have long since embrac'd. But his Familiarity inspir'd in me further Distrust, & I could sense the living Rocks beating as dispers'd Clumps of my own Heart. (807-808)

At that point, Karl's wariness of strangers is the product of a mother's affinity for her children's welfare, and so he decides to "destroy Darwin & the Others, burning their Bodies in the Ship from whence they issu'd" (809).

However, Karl is not a murderer, and his adopted kinsfolk are not readily prone to violence either. The foreigners make camp with Karl and eat the combustible crabs they catch near the rock-bird-humans. As Karl relates, "Miraculously, the Crabs did not detonate in their Mouths, which germinat'd in me the Judgement that Men dampen the Magick of Existence, & that those living Rocks were not living after all, but as Dead as those in the dreary Village I hail'd from" (810). Even with this awareness, Karl befriends Darwin, admiring his "Fascination with the false Fauna." All is going well when, as night begins to fall,

a rogue Band of Four Gore-borns emerg'd, descending from the Shadows, & stabb'd a few of Darwin's Companions in an attempt to eradicate the Mole Invad'rs, but ere they could slay Darwin & the rest, the Fowl Lord manifest'd, who, Five Meters in Height, possess'd the full Body of a Condor, the Neck of a Swan, the Head & Face of a Man, & the Eyes of a Hawk. Most Regal was His Hair, which was the Tail of a Peacock, like a Chieftain's Headdress. They cower'd in His Presence, but, with Resolve, the murderous Rogues swoop'd toward the Fowl Lord, & with a single Wave of His Wing He smote Them all. (823)

Believing the crabmeat to be tainted, all but Darwin board the ship in mortal fear of the hallucination they witnessed. However,

Karl allows the inquisitive Darwin a keyhole-shaped glimpse into the islands' secrets, an inkling of truth patched with excuses and fabrications. It is correct to say that Karl indeed develops a bit of trust toward the fellow naturalist, who later refers to him fondly as a "supernaturalist," but the potential dangers of full disclosure were too great. Thus, an implicit, although obfuscated, knowledge grows between them, and they continue to correspond long after Darwin's departure, communicating by way of magnetic bottles, which, when tossed into the sea, could find any shore or ship deck that supported the feet of his friend. Along with messages of a personal nature, Karl divulges just enough information, albeit encoded and amalgamated, to produce Darwin's great observations and theories, with any inaccuracies the product of a necessary opacity.

Regardless, the momentous visitation of the *Beagle* helped foster in Karl a festering suspicion, at times a loathing, of human beings, which further complicates not only his relationship with Darwin, but his perception of the outside world as a whole. Tensions, too, increase between the bird-humans and their incarnadine counterparts, who attempt several more coups against the Fowl Lord, all ending in their butchery. On a night when the Fowl Lord assumes that he executed the last of the insurrectionists, claiming to have "clipp'd the wicked Wings of Mutiny," Karl writes:

> With the Facsimile of Flight inevitable in Man's Progress, my Bird-humans, my Kin, will surely be imperil'd. The dim Shadow of Man is visibly ruffling Their Feathers. Yet They seem prepar'd for It, prophetic in the Belief that They will rise & dive, dive & rise. Half of Their Quantity schemes to construct spherical Nests of Wind & Air with the Scope of Cities, adapting to Life at the nethermost Region of the Sea, Their Wings twisting into stunning Fins. (830)

When contemplating this underwater nation, Karl compares them with the winged fish and mermaids he heard tell of (perhaps aboard the unnamed British schooner). Flying, he thought, was not exclusive to air, but with the right adjustment could occur in any and all elements. Regarding the rest of the population:

> They have been tempering Themselves in the Fringes of the

Atmosphere, predicting the Chill will crystalize Their Skin into Something Metallurgic, & then They will fly higher, nesting in Craters on the Moon, in Spots on the Sun, & Yonder. These are Dwellings in which Man will eternally be one Step behind, but whose pertinacious Progress will eventually force my Bird-humans to fly-swim ever Downward, ever Upward, ever Onward. (831)

Over the course of his studies, a romance ensues between Karl and a bird-human. This not only convolutes his perceptions further, but might have contributed to the alteration of his existence:

> In the Beginning, the Females were prone to a social Snub of my Presence, save for a Female who seem'd Herself an Outcast, although not of the crimson Complexion, not Gore-born. She, my darling ¡Vhinda, spent most of Her Time perch'd in the Trees or transfix'd by the tantalizing Stars, gripping the edge of a cliff on the Island's south Side so that She may sense both the speckl'd Void above and the wet World below.... Only She had been Audacious enough to lip-peck the nova-shap'd Seeds from my quivery, scarr'd Palm, once even permitting me to Stroke the Top of her felt Wing, reminding me, oddly enough, of a high quality Fez of Turkey that a Man in my Village donn'd. (951-952)

Following this are several chapters in which he worries and envisions the extinction of the winged beings, wondering and dreading if that Turkish headwear he knew of was not indeed manufactured from the wings of his creatures. He describes multiple dreams that are clones of each other, plus or minus minor distinctions:

> O, They came to me. They had only me. I would have murder'd whomever committ'd such a demoniacal Deed. My wing'd Family, reduc'd to a dying Crawl. O, They crawl'd, Scores of Them, Their Claws rending the Soil & Sand, edging toward me, the entirety of Them wingless, with twin Geysers of hazel Blood flying forth from Their Backs. O, flying! All that flew was Their Lives, Rivers at a time, Rivers & Rivers of

depleting Life. (979)

The dreams were the byproduct of a fever caused by Karl's metamorphosis. His bones were becoming more hollow, his jutting lips thinner and harder, and his shoulder blades ached with emerging cartilage, which were, like a goat's horn buds, the beginning of wings. The bird-humans' consensus was that love acted as the ultimate shamanic potion, or, rather, as an antidote to the anthropological curse. Like a dying man who holds within his head mere scriptural knowledge of paradise, Karl was both fearful of his transformation, at times considering it an illness, and enthralled by it, wondering if he wasn't passing into a different type of hereafter, a region of divinity populated by appointed avifauna.

Before the initial signs of his change, Karl and ¡Vhinda attempt to copulate, to perform a soul-dive. "She clutch'd my Hands and sent me aflight, leading me in that sidereal Dance, around & around, cradling me as I enter'd Her and we soul-div'd, enwrapp'd in Wind" (1,307). But the resulting child was stillborn, with random body parts belonging to either the anatomy of a bird or a human: "The lower Lip the Bottom of a Beak, the Hair as serpentine Feathers, one shrunken Wing, & a chicken-clubb'd Foot" (1,333). As far as is revealed, they did not try again, even after the completion of his metamorphosis, although they did sometimes fantasize about the fertility of their innards, the incubatory power of their insides if turned outward. Suicide as nativity.

Yet Karl's heart was indeed a nest, and during his life it begat many symbolic birds, including one in the form of understanding both the overt and clandestine influence of *Homo sapiens avis* on our society, which we are only just beginning to fathom. Perhaps, camouflaged, they live among us, betrayed by reports of invisible wings bending the light behind politicians' backs, although this has not been confirmed. Unfortunately, the extent of such overall influences, concrete or abstract, is limited by deleterious effects. The reason for this is DNA's envy, the irresolvable discrepancy of the winged and the not, which is epitomized in the following: there existed a nameless scientist, perhaps a descendant of Darwin, who, extrapolating from the texts of his keyhole knowledge, attempted to recreate a kind of bird-human. All that remains of his work is crazed, haphazard jottings about the process, and a photograph of what some believe is a patient, others the scientist himself, cowering in the corner with bony wings stitched to an oozing back (Mingles 641-666). In the context of Erasmus Karl's work, we can view this image as, not irrefutable evidence of the creatures' existence, but a demonstration of a universal truth within us: we, the wingless beings, envy those with the power of aviation separate from supplementary invention; we long to join in communion with the invisible, omnipresent flock and forever migrate from the woes of terrestrial life, but we cannot.

~

Bibliography

Boris of Aventaria. *The Purloined Philosophia*. Medieval Science and Philosophy Series, London, 1991. 56.

In the Sky of the Tesseractyles. Dir. Absolon Dubois. Prod. Javier Macron. 1898.

Karl, Erasmus. *The Nidificant Manuscript: The Untold Story of our Winged Relatives*. TT Books, New York, 2019.

Kinbote, Darrell. "Man on the Moon Meets Monster?" *U.S.A. (Unscrupulous Sources for America)*. 11.3 (1971): 39.

Krasznahorkai, Timofey. "The Angel Yearning: Deceits and Delusions Regarding Heaven's Servants." *The Periodical of the Viktor Science Institute for Debunking*. 21.9 (1980): 24-59.

Mare, Kate. "The Ineffective Forger: Hoaxes throughout History." *Skeptical Magazine*. 40.4 (2011): 25.

Mast, Norman. "To See the Unseeable: Inferences on Alien Knowledge." *The Cosmic Cortex: A Journal of Ancient Biology & Related Disciplines*. 20.1 (1989): 34.

Mingles, Jarvis. *Again and Again: Failed Experiments Since the Dawn of Science*. Axiom Books, London, 2000. 641-666.

Oro, Hal. *Word of Mouth: Unofficial Reviews and Criticism of Vintage Films*. Shift Publications, New York, 2014. 10, 18-19.

Vātsyāyana. *The Complete Kama Sutra*. Pearl Editions, London, 2017. 69-70.

———

Luisa Sontag holds multiple PhDs from a variety of universities. Her wide range of knowledge is reflected in her published work. For example, her essay on time's golden spiral shape was published in *Quark*, her research on the gene-popping of rare squids was featured in *Subaquatic Studies*, and her six-volume history of vanished continents was published by Samurai Books. Up until his death, she was collaborating with Stephen Hawking on a book about theoretical flora and fauna titled *A Brief Visit to Neighboring Planets*. Dedicated to Hawking, it is scheduled to be published next year.

George Salis is the award-winning author of *Sea Above, Sun Below* (forthcoming from River Boat Books (www.riverboatbooks.com), 2019). His fiction is featured in *The Dark*, *Black Dandy*, *Zizzle Literary Magazine*, *The Sunlight Press*, *Unreal Magazine*, and elsewhere. His criticism has appeared in *Isacoustic*, *Atticus Review*, and *The Tishman Review*, and his science article on the mechanics of natural evil was featured in *Skeptic*. He is the editor of *The Collidescope* and is currently working on an encyclopedic novel titled *Morphological Echoes*. He has taught in Bulgaria, China, and Poland. Find him on Facebook (www.facebook.com/georgesaliswriter), Goodreads (www.goodreads.com/author/show/16518464.George_Salis), and at www.GeorgeSalis.com.

POOR GIRL

An essay by Jackie Rivera, as provided by Traci Castleberry

From across the cobbled street, I watched the rag-clad girl who huddled on the leeward side of the Dolphin Inn. She held one trembling palm extended toward a passing gentleman. "Spare a copper, mister?" The man, like all the other passers-by gave the girl a wide berth, especially when she let out a barrage of coughs.

She was perfect for what I needed. The difficulty breathing was bad enough to be indicative of pneumonia or consumption, either of which would probably kill her soon. From the livid red scar and the fused fingers clutching at the collar of her worn dress, she'd been burned, and not all that long ago. No one would miss her, and she was near enough to death that if she passed on, I wouldn't feel bad.

My missing hand itched as it always did when I was excited. I wound my way through the crowd and crouched in front of her, ignoring the stares of those walking past. "Spare a copper, mister?" she asked me.

I touched the knuckles of my good hand to my cap. "Morning, miss. I don't have a copper, but I do have a hot bowl of stew to fill your belly and a nice warm bed to rest in."

It was hard to make out her expression beneath her dirt-stained face, but her eyes widened as she gazed suspiciously at me. "I don't have nothing you want. I got the consumption. Ain't fit to lie with."

"I don't want to lie with you." I held out my hand. "I'm just trying to be gentlemanly and help the less fortunate."

"You ain't no gentleman."

I inhaled sharply, wondering if this pathetic urchin had guessed the truth I hid beneath my jacket and trousers. Then again, those near death were often delusional. "It's your choice. Come with me or stay out here in the cold." A night on the streets of Whitby was nothing to wish for with the constant threat from the sailors, traders, and dockworkers, as well as the bitter sea wind that almost never stopped.

Another round of coughing left her bent double. When the fit ended, I saw defeat in her eyes. She was so worn and tired that any risk would be better than enduring another moment begging on the street. She accepted my hand. I had to help her rise as she stood on unsteady legs. The poor girl was barefoot, her feet black and thick with calluses, and she shivered when I put an arm around her waist for support. She was hot, feverish, and I wondered more than once if she'd make it to my dwelling, which was not in Whitby proper but hewn into the cliffs below.

There were still a couple of functioning alum mines up north in Boulby, but for the most part the ones in Whitby had been abandoned, leaving me the ideal place to hide. The only time I feared trouble was when overzealous scientists had discovered the fossilized skeleton of a gigantic crocodile and incited searches for more. There were also those searching for veins of jet, the black mineraloid locals carved into crosses and beads and other jewelry. Men and boys scoured the cliffs after each high tide and storm, looking for any veins that might have been exposed. Fortunately, few came near my mine, and when they did, I scared them away with strange noises, letting them think the place haunted.

The main entrance had been sealed up, but I'd found another hidden beneath an overhang, which made it all but invisible from above or below. It was here I guided the girl, who by then had nearly collapsed from exhaustion. I had to catch her when she stumbled, though having her half delirious was to my benefit. The less she was aware of, the less she could reveal later—if she lived to say anything at all.

Once inside, she gazed in childlike wonderment at my furnishing, most of which must have seemed wondrous or foreign to her. She gaped at the ceiling where I'd hung Chinese paper lanterns from the wooden beams. "Pretty," she said. Then she stared at the rest of the furnishings, the mahogany dining set missing only one chair, the shelves lined with books, the bed frame shaped with elegant nautical themes that could only have come from a captain's cabin. "You have everything. How's you get all this stuff in here?"

"I carried it." All of my furnishings had been scavenged from the multitude of shipwrecks along the Yorkshire coast. A few things, like the lanterns, I'd bought from traders. I even had a small, pot-bellied stove, properly ventilated, to cook, heat water, and maintain the main room at a pleasant temperature.

"It's just like a proper home, even if it isn't." She coughed, hard enough that she bloodied the handkerchief she yanked out of her pocket. Poor girl. She wouldn't last much longer.

I guided her over to the bed and sat her down, where she stared at me as if I was something miraculous.

"Why you being so nice?"

"I have my reasons." None of which I was going to tell her. I lifted the kettle from where I'd left it simmering and poured hot water into a mug already prepared with one of my favorite blends. "Here. This will ease your cough."

"Been an awful long time since I had a proper cup of tea." She wrapped her hands around the mug and sipped. She paused with a thoughtful expression. For a moment, I feared she'd tasted the hemp and wouldn't finish, but, no, she was only taking her time and savoring the rare treat.

It wasn't long before the drug took effect. I caught the half-empty mug before it fell from her limp fingers. She slumped over, fast asleep.

I carried her over to the table and laid her out. With a knife I stripped her filthy dress and shawl and tossed them into the stove to burn. Her age was difficult to discern, sixteen, perhaps eighteen, as she was skinny, bony, and covered in flea bites. The burn that had ruined her hand extended all the way up to her shoulder. Despite my intentions to remain aloof, I pitied the girl having ended up so poorly.

Once I scrubbed the dirt and salt from her face, I discovered something. She was pretty. Illness had sucked much of the color from her complexion, but her lips were a soft rose-pink. Her shift did little to hide the curves of her breasts or the shapely legs.

I shook my useless fancies aside. If she were anything like my previous subjects, she wouldn't last the night. With a length of rope, I bound her to the table, no easy task with one wooden hand, but I didn't want her to fall off when she thrashed. That done, I went to fetch my prize.

George screeched at me as soon as I opened the steel door to my workshop. He thrust a fuzzy hand through the bars of his cage and hopped madly until I cut an apple in half and gave it to him. I snatched my fingers back in time to avoid his sharp teeth. I'd bought him off a sailor who'd gone to India and brought back several monkeys. I don't think he forgave me for letting his mate die when I used her to test an elixir to heal wounds. He probably hated me for trying it on him, too, but at least he'd lived.

The table was covered in glass vials, copper tubing, mortars, pestles, and herbs, but my real prize rested inside a golden pot covered with hardened six-and-one mud. The present mixture, one meant to restore balance in the body, had been simmering for nine days and nights, and I couldn't leave it much longer.

Carefully, I poured it into a bowl of pure gold and carried it out to the main room. I lifted the girl's head and held it to her lips. She didn't wake but swallowed the concoction of silver, mercury, and other minerals easily enough. In ordinary circumstances, the mixture would be deadly.

If I'd done everything right, it would cure.

~

I spent the night seated on a cushion and reciting the proper incantations in Chinese. My ghost hand itched and tingled. The pictograms I'd carved into the table seemed to shift and waver, although I dismissed that as fatigue on my part. After a half hour, the girl moaned and started to writhe. I didn't stop speaking, even when her moans increased to terrible screams that echoed throughout the mine.

The sound didn't worry me beyond possible damage to my hearing. It only increased the likelihood of someone thinking the place haunted. Besides, after a while, the screams dulled to a whimper then ceased altogether. I was certain I'd killed her. She'd gone even paler, her breaths almost imperceptibly shallow. I continued to chant fervently, keeping both hope and disappointment at bay. The pictograms twisted and writhed, and for an instant there was ... *something*. An energy, a spirit, I didn't know which, but its presence left my skin warm and tingling.

When the prescribed nine hours had passed, I rose and felt for the pulse in her wrist. It was faint but regular. Her breathing was steady with no sign of consumption.

I dropped her wrist, not quite believing what I saw. The girl had surprised me.

She'd lived.

~

There were numerous ways of disposing of a body, which included burial or hauling it out to sea, but dealing with a live girl was something I hadn't prepared for.

Added to that was the risk that she would leave and expose my work to the wrong people. I could keep George in a cage, but callous though I was, something within me resisted keeping a young woman locked up for the time it would take to prepare the next elixir. A chain would do well enough.

But first, I had only the one bed and I wasn't about to risk it to lice. She was weak and feverish and didn't wake as I untied her. My initial thought was to simply shave her head, as it would have been simpler, but I couldn't bring myself to deprive the girl of a piece of her beauty when she'd nearly died. So I washed it with a potion to kill vermin, dragged the comb through it, and it turned a pretty, pale blond. Then I tucked her into bed, certain she wouldn't wake while her body continued to replenish itself.

After growing up amongst the slaves in Batavia, I loathed the thought of chaining the girl to the bed, but I couldn't risk her escaping. To spare her pretty skin, I wrapped a length of cloth around her ankle so the manacle didn't chafe. It wouldn't do to have her die of infection before the next elixir was ready.

The excitement of the night had left me wide awake. I hurried into town, passing through the marketplace to pick up a loaf of bread and other essentials, and then to a modest store on Church Street. It was rarely busy; the locals tended to distrust foreigners like Xiao Liu unless they were desperate.

But I was neither a local nor desperate and headed right in. The store, made fragrant by hundreds of dried herbs, was empty except for Xiao Liu, who stood behind the counter grinding some dried leaves in a mortar. As soon as he saw me, he poured two cups of tea, as was our tradition. "You're up early," he said in Chinese.

"I'm out of arsenolite," I said, preferring our own language to English. The tea was one of Xiao Liu's blends to calm the mind and had a faint, fruity flavor.

"Poisoning rats again?" Xiao Liu's raised eyebrow indicated he knew I was doing anything but.

"I need it for the six-and-one." Alum, soapstone, oyster, and salt I had no need of buying, since I could find them in the mine or nearby, but the arsenolite was not native to England and had to be imported. I needed a few herbs too and passed him a list.

Xiao Liu glanced at the items then rummaged through the hundreds of drawers lining his wall. "And what are you concocting this time? A cure for the lepers at the hospital?"

He was always suggesting something altruistic for me to do. I hadn't taken him up on the offer. "My hand is bothering me. I'm having trouble sleeping."

Xiao Liu frowned. He was my friend and I hated lying to him, but neither could I admit the truth. "Does it hurt?" he asked, genuinely concerned.

I nodded, not trusting myself to say anything. My missing hand did cause me pain on occasion, but not enough to keep me awake.

"Let me see."

I pushed up my left sleeve to the elbow and unbuckled the leather straps that secured the wooden hand to the stump at my wrist. Xiao Liu poked and prodded, muttered something to himself then brought out his dish of fine needles and inserted a few into points along my arm. After a few breaths, the phantom itching eased. I let my arm rest while he went about collecting the herbs I needed and organizing them into paper packets.

Finished, he removed the needles and massaged my arm and shoulder. He put a new supply of lamb's wool between the hand and my stump and buckled it on, checking the fit as he did so. "Feel better?"

"Yes, teacher. Thank you." I set a few coins down, but when I reached for my supplies with my good hand, he grabbed my wrist and set his fingertips on my pulse.

"Tell me the truth, Jackie. What are you up to?"

"I—" Arguing was useless. So was escape. Xiao Liu could break my wrist with little effort. "Testing an elixir. On monkeys." Human ones, but I didn't dare say that.

"Which elixir?"

"The one meant to restore balance to the body."

He let go, but his gaze was hard. "When you were my apprentice, you had all the makings of a good physician. Your mind is bright. These are gifted hands." He took both my palms and turned them upward. "But you lack compassion. You keep your heart locked away."

I jerked out of his grip, stung by the reminder of why Xiao Liu had dismissed me. I didn't care. I'd learned enough to experiment on my own, and Xiao Liu wouldn't approve of what I meant to do. My skin tingled. He'd struck closer than I'd hoped. "Goodbye, teacher. Thank you for your assistance." I collected my packets and tucked them into various pockets.

"If you're working evil, the spirits will know. They will turn on you."

I left the shop without looking back. The tingling didn't stop until I reached the market.

~

When I returned laden with parcels, the girl was awake. She hadn't moved from the bed, but she watched me organize my packages. "I bought some fresh ox tail and vegetables at the market. I'll make a stew. I promised you that."

"Am I your prisoner?" The chain jangled as she kicked.

"For now." I had no reason to lie to her.

She lay passively as I sliced meat and carrots and set the pot over the stove to cook. "What's wrong with your hand?"

"It's missing." I held up my wooden appendage so she could see it better.

Her chin dropped. "How'd that happen?"

"None of your business." I wasn't in the mood for stories. To my relief, she asked nothing else while I finished preparing dinner. Once I had the stew simmering, I went over to her and asked, "How do you feel?"

"Ain't never felt better. Almost like I was cured."

"That's because you are." I checked her pulse just to be sure. Strong and regular, just like her breathing.

"How? You didn't use leeches or bleed me or nothing."

"Why would I rob your body of something it needs?" I examined her hand, the burned one, mentally going through the recipes in my book of elixirs and thinking of which ones I might try. "English doctors have a lot to learn about balance within a body."

"You ain't English, are you? Your eyes is different and you talk strange."

I should have cut out her tongue when I had the chance. "I was born in Batavia. My mother was Chinese. My father was Portuguese."

Her eyes grew big. "Do you speak Chinese? Will you say something?"

I was fluent in Chinese, Portuguese, Spanish, and English and knew a smattering of Dutch and French, although I didn't tell her that. It must have been her innocent fascination that moved me, but I recited a poem I'd learned in childhood. She had no idea what it meant but clapped her hands in delight. "It's pretty. Say something else."

"Later. I have a few things to take care of while the stew cooks. Rest for a while and then we'll eat, all right?"

She pouted, but she was still too tired to leave the bed. I grabbed my packets of herbs and arsenolite and hurried off to the workshop where George greeted me with another screech of rage.

"Shut up, you." I tossed another apple to him. In the other cages, the doves and rats clamored for their dinner as well. I fed them all, and at last could turn my attention to my mixture. The six-and-one mud would take a month to prepare. In the meantime, I had to figure out what to do with my unexpected guest.

~

The girl held her spoon awkwardly in her damaged hand as she downed her dinner. I wondered when she'd eaten last, but she hadn't complained during the long wait for the stew to cook. "I don't know what to call you." She sat on the edge of the bed, legs swinging, the chain going *clink-clink-clink*.

I had half a mind to yank her onto the floor to stop the din. "Jackie will do."

"I'm Violet. At least, that's what Milady called me. She liked all her maids to have flower names." She wrinkled he nose. "It's better than the name Mama gave me, though."

Since she obviously expected me to ask, I said, "Which was?"

106

"Harriet."

She was right. Violet suited her better.

"You get a lot of visitors?"

There was a note of worry in her voice. "No one comes down here. They think this mine is haunted."

Violet paled and went still. "Is it?"

I shrugged. "It's true there was a cave-in and twelve men died, but if their spirits are hanging about, I haven't seen them."

"Oh, Jackie, I don't like ghosts." She shivered. "I'm scared of the dark."

I bit back annoyance at her childish behavior. "I'll leave a lantern burning, all right?"

I did just that when it was time for bed. I could have evicted my patient but decided it wasn't worth the effort. I collected a few blankets and a pillow and made do on the ground. The chain rattled as Violet made herself comfortable. She patted the mattress. "There's room for two."

"I'm fine here." I could sleep anywhere and wake rested.

"You sleeping there 'cause I'm sick or 'cause you want me thinking you're a man?"

Her observation struck me dumb for a few moments. I had to fight to keep my composure.

"I knows who you are," she said sleepily. "You're Jacqueline Rivera. You killed your husband and stowed away on a ship where you pretended to be a man. You turned pirate, but it wasn't treasure you wanted, it was books. The English captured your ship but you escaped. The butler read us your story from the paper."

The girl was too keen by far. I should have altered my name more than I had, but since it worked as a male moniker, I'd kept it. "Don't believe everything you hear. Jacqueline Rivera's husband was a lecherous lout more than twice her age. Now she's dead too. She jumped overboard and drowned."

"They never found her body."

"It's a big ocean."

"Do you miss being on a ship?"

My missing hand suddenly ached with a sharp, burning agony akin to that of the day I'd lost it. Crippled as I was, I couldn't return to the sea I craved, and I hated the girl for reminding me of what I couldn't have. "Go to sleep. If you don't, I'll give you a draught so deep you won't wake until next week."

She watched as I readied my blankets and pillows on the floor. "Do you dress like a man because you don't like being a girl? I mean, I knows you can't be a girl on a ship, but why do you dress like that on land?"

There were several females serving openly on other ships, but I didn't bother arguing. I wondered if she'd always been so observant or if her brush with death had heightened her senses. "Shut your mouth before I do it for you."

I glanced back at her, glaring, but she gazed resolutely at me. Sighing, I kept my back to her, stripped off my shirt and unwound the lengths of cloth I used to bind my breasts. The relief was worth feeling her stare.

"You're awful pretty, Jackie."

My ghost hand throbbed. I pulled up the covers without looking at her.

~

It must have been past midnight when Violet's trembling voice woke me. "Jackie? The ghosts ain't gonna come, are they?"

Damn the stupid girl. "There are no ghosts. I told you."

Silence stretched. The chain clinked, then, "Jackie? I'm too scared to sleep alone."

I sighed. I should never have told her about the cave-in, but I'd forgotten how frightened the young could be.

"Please, Jackie?"

Figuring I'd never get to sleep if she kept pestering me, I climbed in next to her. She was soft and snuggled against me like a puppy. When she curled an arm around my waist, I stiffened. I'd never had any desire to lie with a man, but I wasn't entirely comfortable this close to a woman, either.

"It's all right," she whispered. "I used to share a bed with Rose, before—"

Before the fire had put her out of a job. I didn't ask for details. I didn't want to know.

But then she began to cry, a choking, muffled sound that turned into a sob and dampened my shoulder. I lay there stiffly with no idea how to comfort a hysterical female.

It turned out I didn't need to do a thing. Between gasping breaths, she did the talking. "It were my fault. Milady's brother ...

he went to sea and had just come back. He'd been out for a long time with no womenfolk."

It wasn't hard to guess where this was going.

"He came in my room carrying a lamp. He put his hands on me and I—" She took a long, shuddering breath. "I kicked him. He dropped the lamp. The bedclothes caught, and then the curtain, and he was burning and screaming. I would've burned, too, if Mr. Jenks hadn't fetched me out of there."

"The butler?"

"Aye. He was a good man, was Mr. Jenks. Always looking out for us. But even he were too late. Milady's brother died. Half the house burned before they could put the fire out. Milady let me go, she did. Called me such awful names when I tried to tell her what happened. It were terrible, watching him die."

Terrible for her, perhaps. I'd killed men, including my husband, but seeing their life drain away had left me with an intense satisfaction.

"Will you hold me, Jackie?"

I didn't care to. I wanted my nest on the floor where I could curl up alone and forget she was here, but the calculating part of me was curious as to what it would take to make the girl stop trembling. After so many years at sea and living alone, femininity was a mystery to me, and I was never one to let a puzzle go unsolved.

So I rolled over. She pressed against me, her slight figure warm against mine and not altogether uncomfortable. I swept her hair aside and rubbed her back through the thin cotton shift. I fingered each bone in her spine, taking in the curve of her body.

And later, when she kissed me, I didn't resist.

~

As was my habit, I woke early and went out to walk the shoreline. I needed the smell of the salt air, much as it hurt to watch the ships come and go with supplies. I wanted to be out there with them but I couldn't, not until I was able to restore my hand.

The past few days had been calm so I didn't expect to find any usable scraps washed ashore. I was right on that account, but I did find a pair of ammonites. The locals called them snakestones after a legend in which Saint Hilda had rid the area of snakes by turning them to stone. I tucked them in my pocket, wondering if Violet had ever seen one.

When I returned, the iron door to my workshop stood ajar with a length of chain leading inside. Fury pinched my temples as I followed the trail of links. Violet, dressed in a patched shirt over her shift, stood in front of George's cage. The door was open.

"Leave it alone!"

She swiveled around. The monkey was in her arms, his fingers curled in her hair. "He's very sweet. Wherever did you find him?"

"He's a vicious little creature that—"

George hissed and bared his teeth. Violet cooed to him, and to my shock he settled down. I took the hint and left him alone. After all, I didn't care whether he befriended Violet. The less I had to do with him, the better.

"What are you doing in here?"

She waved a dust rag at me. "This place ain't bad for a mine, but it could use some tidying up."

I couldn't disagree. Housekeeping was never a priority and it was impossible to be rid of the dust. "Did you touch this?" I pointed to my iron pot of six-and-one.

"No." She gazed at it. "What is it?"

"It doesn't matter. Go near it, and I'll cut off your good hand."

She didn't seem fazed by my threat. Instead, her eyes widened. "Is that a magic potion? Is that what you used to cure me?"

"It's not magic. It's science. A simple mixture involving complex preparation."

"I gets it." She gestured to the bowls, jars and vials upon the table. "I was a good lady's maid. Milady had me make all her creams and lotions. I know a good one for making hands smooth. Smells like peaches."

The last thing I needed was smelly concoctions for fancy women. "You're too young to be a lady's maid."

Violet hung her head. "I wasn't, but Milady's maid Rose taught me how to act proper and all that. I stood in for Rose sometimes." She scratched George's head, and he chittered in pleasure. "I'll help you. I'll do anything you want. Mix, grind, stir, cook, clean, you just ask."

George's adoration—and consequent good behavior—was enough for me to tolerate her presence. "Fine. But clean the main room first. I've got work to do."

She hurried out, George perched on her shoulder.

As she'd boasted, she was a deft hand at mixing draughts, lotions, and anything else I might require. Besides that, she was an excellent cook and housekeeper but never touched my equipment unless I asked her to.

"If you let me go out, I'll sell the potions for you. I swears I won't betray you," she told me one night while we were in bed together. "I likes it here with you."

Of course she did. She nowhere else to go. I provided her with plenty of food, shelter, and the possibility of earning an income. That sort of independence was something I understood and didn't want to discourage.

"But if I goes out, I needs a dress. I can't wear this." She tugged at her shift.

A dress. Part of me recoiled at the thought of even touching such a garment, but she was right. She couldn't go out in a shift and old shirt, and she was far too feminine to wear boy's clothes. "I'll see what I can do."

"I want a blue one. Blue as the sky."

So I went into town and stopped at a shop that sold castoffs from rich families. Most were too fancy and would attract too much attention, but there was a day dress of blue muslin I hoped would work. Not knowing what possessed me, I bought a hair ribbon to match.

She was thrilled and tried it on right there in front of me. "Needs some taking in, but it's perfect, Jackie. I never had no better."

I had to admit it suited her. The bodice was moderately low and hugged her breasts. Her hair was pulled back in a braid and tied with the ribbon so her pale shoulders were exposed. The only thing out of place was the chain, and that I removed. "Run, and I will hunt you down. Betray my secrets, and you'll regret it."

"I won't." She stood on tiptoe and kissed my cheek. "Just you wait. I knows the market, I does."

~

And so she proved true to her word.

She turned out to be a shrewd bargainer, and once she convinced me to make herbal cures, started selling or trading them along with her lotions in exchange for food or supplies. Often, she took George, who ended up being a great draw for children and their parents and earning a few additional coins.

I suppose I looked on her presence as an experiment in itself. I'd been around women so rarely that I was fascinated by the way she moved and the kindness with which she treated George.

Strange, how I could admire in another that which I hated in myself. I loved to watch her bathe, as she sat in the tub and let the water trickle through her hair and between her breasts. When I took my turn in the water, I arranged a folding screen around the tub as a hint I didn't want to be disturbed.

She ignored it.

She dashed around the screen, cloth in one hand, bottle of one of her smelly concoctions in the other. I just had time to grab a towel and wrap it around myself. "Get the hell out of here!"

Playfully, she tried to pluck the towel from me so she could play the lady's maid and wash me, but I caught her good wrist and dug my fingers deep. "Leave me alone."

She sucked in her lower lip, and for a moment I was afraid she was going to cry. I couldn't stand weepy females. Then her gaze dropped to where my left arm ended. "Tell me what happened."

Cursing, I let her go and stepped out of the tub, hiding the stump beneath the towel's folds. Her curves, visible through her thin cotton shift, made me uncomfortably aware of my bony, damaged body. "Cannonball." The loss of my hand wasn't the extent of it, just the worst.

She rubbed her wrist. I'd probably bruised it. "It must've hurt."

I'd just turned to gather my clothes when she took my arm. I was too stunned to thrust her away. In bed we'd both worn clothes so I'd had an extra layer of protection. Now I had no defenses, and I hated being helpless. I'd fought and killed men armed with pistols and sabers. I'd survived storms, battles and a long swim to shore, yet this wispy girl I'd found on the streets held me captive with touch alone.

"Come on, Jackie."

She took my good hand in her thin fingers and led me to the bed. I sat hunched over while her soft fingers worked at the towel.

"I'm not afraid to look."

Perhaps not, but I was afraid to let her. Eventually, her kindness wore me down. Eyes closed, I told her how a cannonball had struck the *Santa Isabella*. Wood had gone flying. Several large splinters had driven into my flesh. The biggest one had gone through my palm and shattered most of the bones. The *Santa Isabella* was captured by the English and the wounded transferred to their ship. The surgeon had cut off my hand at the wrist and cauterized the stump, but once he'd seen I was female, I knew my career was over.

I wouldn't let the captain hang me or turn me over to the authorities, so I'd jumped overboard and clung to a piece of flotsam until I reached English shores. The cold and the salt water kept my wound fever at bay, but once I climbed onto dry land, illness struck hard. If Xiao Liu hadn't found me, I would no doubt have died in the local hospital. Instead, he laid me on a cot in the back of his shop and tended my wounds with remedies thousands of years old. Once the fever passed, he gave me strengthening exercises and taught me the rudiments of Chinese medicine.

Violet listened with rapt fascination. She traced my scars with her fingers. "You're amazing, Jackie."

Her shift joined my towel on the floor. What followed was an experiment and all in the name of science. My reactions. Hers. How this touch made her moan and that one made her wriggle. I didn't mind the warmth of her body against mine, though I felt none of the enjoyment she seemed to as I ran my hands over her naked flesh and delved into her deepest parts. I let her touch me, kiss me, probe me, but my heart remained as cold as it had when I was Xiao Liu's apprentice.

I felt nothing beyond the physical. I couldn't.

The next elixir would soon be ready.

~

I didn't want to deal with any protests Violet might have, so I dosed her tea with a light sedative. While she was dazed, I urged her onto the table, removed her pretty blue dress and tied an elaborately-knotted rope around her. I made sure her damaged arm was exposed up to the shoulder where the burn ended.

George hopped and shrieked, alternately trying to bite me and pawing at Violet's motionless body. I finally had to grab the creature by the back of his neck and thrust him into his cage, which he hadn't used in weeks. The screeching increased, muted only when I slammed the iron door shut.

"Jackie?" Violet's voice trembled. She was afraid, but it couldn't be helped. "Jackie, what are you doing?"

"I'm going to fix your hand."

At this she awakened fully. "It don't need fixing! Please, Jackie. Please leave it alone."

I ignored her protest and brought over the bowl. The liquid, while still warm, was no longer hot. "It's meant to return a body to its true form." Carefully, I poured it down the length of her arm and pooled most of it on her damaged hand and fingers.

For several moments, nothing happened. Then she tensed, and a wail broke from her throat. "Take it off, Jackie! Take it off! It burns!"

She jerked and thrashed. Tears slid down her cheeks. I could have used acupuncture and herbs for the pain but I didn't. The dark part of my soul wanted to be certain I could watch her suffer and remain unaffected. "It's only for nine hours."

This brought a renewed barrage of pleas and screams. "Jackie! Jackie, *please!*"

I took my seat on the cushion and repeated the incantations to go with this new elixir. After a while, I couldn't take the screaming. I stuffed a gag into her mouth, ignoring the tears and look of betrayal.

If she hadn't been tied down, I'm sure she would have torn at her own flesh, but my sailor's knots held true and she was helpless to free herself. It took over two hours for her strength to fail. By then, she was a sodden, sweaty mess, exhausted and trembling.

I continued my chanting. As before, the words wriggled and twisted on the table. I had the vague awareness of shadows flitting back and forth, darting in and out of the mixture drying on Violet's hand.

Spirits. The creatures brushed against me, too, but instead of a tingle, they pinched and burned before they flew away.

I resisted the urge to rub my arm, wondering if the violence had been a threat ... or a promise.

~

Come morning, I rose to check on my patient. The mixture had hardened around her hand and I had to use a knife to peel it away, but there, like a butterfly emerging from its chrysalis, I revealed healthy pink flesh and five separate fingers. I examined each of them, bending every joint to ensure functionality. Violet stared at me with such hatred that I shuddered.

"Look. Your hand is perfect. Just like new." I plucked the gag from her mouth then worked at untying the multitude of knots.

"You *hurt* me." Her voice was barely a whisper. She sat up and glared at me. "You hurt me and you didn't care."

I had her untied. "But your hand—"

"Bully my hand!" She used it to strike me across the face.

My cheek stung. I should have put the chain on her to keep her from leaving, but I couldn't seem to move. I watched as she dressed and packed her few belongings into a satchel. Then she went into my workshop and returned with George in her arms. He hissed and spat as they passed me on the way to the exit. Neither looked back.

I didn't care if she hated me. In childhood and at sea, I'd learned never to love, never to trust. Death was always with us, whether from illness, injury or drowning. And since I had more to hide than others, I kept to myself as much as possible.

It didn't matter that I'd grown used to her presence and would miss her idle chatter. Within a month, I would be back at sea.

I would be whole.

~

Unencumbered by my guest, I went about preparing my next, and last, elixir. I opened the cages for the rats and doves and set them free. They fled, just as Violet had.

I had enough ingredients from the last batch of six-and-one that I didn't need to visit Xiao Liu. I'd also collected the necessary minerals for the elixir itself. Gold. Mercury. Arsenic.

When the mud was ready, I coated the golden crucible and put in the elixir's ingredients. For nine days and nights it brewed. I scrawled Chinese characters into the ground around the fire and myself. I chanted and sang and fasted, drinking only water. I alternated various breathing exercises and meditations, focusing on the success of the experiment.

I refused to let it fail.

On the tenth morning, I lifted the crucible from the fire with shaking hands. I removed the wooden hand then stripped and lay naked on the table amidst the graven characters. I had a rope ready and secured my legs, waist and my shortened arm. With my free hand I poured half the bowl's contents over my stump. The rest of the elixir I drank. It was hot, slippery and filled my mouth with an acidic, metallic taste. My belly churned, protesting the poisonous brew.

I clamped a stick between my teeth then tucked my hand into a small noose and pulled it tight. I was trapped, unable to free myself until I regained sense enough to do so. For a few moments, I reveled in the fact that I'd done it. Whatever came of this elixir, I'd poured my heart and soul and will into it.

Then the pain came.

At first, it was a heat within my belly and a light burn on my skin as if I'd been in the sun too long. Then the brew sunk into my flesh and guts and turned excruciating.

I bit hard on the stick and let out a scream. Every nerve had caught fire. I'd thought Violet weak for enduring her pain so poorly, but now that I experienced it for myself, I knew just how terrible it was. Like childbirth, I tried to tell myself. Hundreds of thousands of women had suffered when they used their bodies to create something new and had been just fine.

I didn't care to remember that thousands more had died in their attempt to bring a new life to completion.

I twisted and writhed atop the table, yanking hard at the rope as my muscles twitched and jerked by their own accord. The characters on the table twisted into deformed parodies of themselves, and I was certain it was my own fevered brain seeing things that weren't there.

Until I felt ... *them*.

Spirits. Hundreds. Thousands of them. They flitted and poked and jeered. Their breath burned my skin. Other drove beneath my flesh, ripping and rending. Agony blinded me. I screamed, but the sound was distant.

Xiao Liu was right. The spirits had turned on me. The elixir proclaimed that by drinking it I could transcend to my true nature, but this was no angelic lifting of the spirit or transformation into the body I craved.

This was hell.

~

I must have clawed myself free of my restraints. Anguish drove me out of my cave and into the open air. Bitter sea wind raked my naked flesh, but I didn't care. I roamed the shore, barefoot, heedless of the sharp black rocks. I was red and ragged and burned, but the truest shock came when I gazed where my arm had once ended.

I had a hand, but I could not call it such. A paw was closer. It was a frightening, ugly thing, covered with the bristled fur of a boar and bearing claws as sharp as a hawk's. The skin was tough as old leather and just as impermeable. The rest of me was covered in burns and blisters that stung with the merest touch of cool air.

The elixir had transformed me into what I truly was: a monster.

I howled my fury. The sound echoed against the cliffs and mingled with the loud rushing of waves. Seagulls shrieked in response. I lashed at one too slow or stupid to get out of my way. It fell in a spray of blood and feathers.

The sea would never be mine again. No crew would take a deformed creature like me aboard. I was worse than female. I was ... inhuman.

I dropped to my hands and knees and raked the sand. Hatred and disappointment burned as deeply as my skin. I'd failed. I deserved it. Years of preparation. Dozens of deaths, both human and animal.

All for nothing.

"Jackie?"

I struck before the voice registered. Hot blood spattered my face and arm. I licked the coppery fluid from my lips.

Then someone screamed.

I thrust the heels of my hands against my ears, but I couldn't shut out her anguish. The sound went on and on. I raised my paw, ready to silence the screamer for good.

Teeth sank into the back of my neck. I yelped and swiped at the little beast, but it was too fast. It darted away, and it was the pain coupled with the sheer incongruity of seeing a monkey scampering on a shell-strewn beach that reached past the feral madness that had taken over my soul.

And then I caught a glimpse of blond hair trailing over a sky-blue dress.

Violet dropped to her knees. The screams turned to moans of pain as she clasped her hands around her belly. Red leaked from between her arms and fingers, trickling down to join the wet sand in soaking her skirt.

"Violet?" The word emerged cracked and broken. My fury disappeared beneath a sudden terror. I didn't have to see the wound to know it was bad. With that much blood, it couldn't be anything else.

I don't know how she managed to smile, but she did. "I brought you back, Jackie. Took me a while but I figured out what you was up to. Came back to stop you, I did."

"It's too late."

"Ain't never too late." She keeled over.

"*Violet!*" I dove toward her. Blood kept coming, running from her belly in torrents. She was dying. I'd killed her after all.

George screeched and pranced, leaving little monkey-prints in the sand. I'd already murdered one female he'd cared for. I'd be damned if I let another die.

I scooped her up and held her against my body as I hurried up the switchback trail leading to the top of the cliff. "Keep your hands there. Press hard," I told her, and she whimpered.

I must have been a frightening sight, naked, blood-covered and carrying the girl I'd just maimed. I didn't care. For once, George didn't screech at me. He wrapped his furry arms around my neck and hung on as I raced toward Xiao Liu's shop.

I didn't have to knock. He was already at the door, probably alerted by the commotion rustling through the street. He waved me inside.

"Here, Jackie." He swept an arm across his counter, abruptly clearing it of bowls, herb packets, and a pair of unlit candles.

I set her down, watching dumbly as Xiao Liu ripped her dress apart to expose the wound. Her intestines glistened. "How?" he asked.

I held up the inhuman thing at the end of my arm.

Xiao Liu didn't reprimand me, but his gaze was accusatorial enough. "Put on a robe. You're going to help me."

"I can't." It galled me to say it. I was a monster, now. Unfit for human company. I headed toward the door. Better that I leave now before I hurt someone else.

I heard sympathy beneath his unhappiness. "Prove the sprits wrong. For that matter, prove yourself wrong."

Even George had gone silent. He sat on the counter, picking at Violet's hair. "I wanted to go back to sea. That's all I ever wanted." To be part of a crew. To have a place in the world where what I could do mattered more than what I was or where I'd come from.

"Hurt or heal, Jackie. What will your choice be?"

She was pale, golden hair sticky and red as her life ebbed away. Twice before I'd been willing to let her die. I'd had nothing to lose. This time, I did.

I took a robe from behind the counter and slid it on. The silk cooled my burns. "Tell me what to do."

~

There was no six-and-one mud this time, no mixtures of mercury and arsenic and gold. Just Xiao Liu's expert hands as he used his acupuncture needles to minimize pain around the wound.

My talons had an unexpected benefit; the tips were as fine as Xiao Liu's needles. I dug them gently into points used to induce sleep while Xiao Liu rinsed the gash. Violet's twitching slowed to something more manageable, allowing Xiao Liu to work unhindered. Remembering how much Violet had enjoyed hearing me recite Chinese poetry and children's tales, I called several to mind and spoke softly as Xiao Liu used silken thread to piece together what I had so callously torn apart.

I spent days and nights at her side, waiting, hoping, changing the poultices and dosing her with draughts to ease the pain. When wound fever turned her body heated and raw, I fretted and bathed her with cool water. I kept my vile hand hidden, unable to lay eyes upon the method of Violet's destruction.

Xiao Liu watched me with the same intensity as I did Violet. "You would make a good physician," he said.

I laughed bitterly. "I've killed men without regret. I didn't care what happened to Violet. I'm a cold, unfeeling creature. I always will be." George screeched softly. I knew he'd agree.

Gently, Xiao Liu drew back my sleeve to expose my disfigured hand. I longed to snatch it back, but I was afraid I'd hurt him, too. "You might have a man's soul, but not an animal's. This," he said with a slight shake of my hand, "is not who you are. Each of us has darkness inside. Don't let it swallow you whole."

I met his gaze. Something inside me cracked. "I'm sorry. For everything."

"I know." He patted my hand and left me alone.

Two days later, Violet's fever broke. The following morning, she opened her eyes and focused on me. She raised a shaky hand and brushed my cheek. "Jackie?"

For the first time since I was a child, I wept.

~

Two weeks later Xiao Liu suggest we go out for a walk. I still refused to wear feminine attire, so Xiao Liu lent me a cotton shirt, pants, and cap, which brought out my Chinese heritage. Between that and the ever-present George, Violet and I earned more than a few stares as we walked to the end of Church Street and up the nearly two hundred stairs to St. Mary's Church and the ruins of Whitby Abbey. Violet clung to my arm from weakness, but she was determined to reach the top. Once there, I led her through the church's graveyard to a bench overlooking the sea. For a long time, the only sounds were the wind and the distant roar of the waves.

When Violet broke the silence, her voice was bitter. "I suppose you'll go back to the sea, now that I'm well."

"No." I clenched my paw, careful of the sharp claws. "I can't."

"You got what you deserved, and I ain't sorry for being glad about it. Not after what you done."

I couldn't refute this, so I didn't.

"It ain't so much that you almost killed me, but you didn't care. I didn't matter no more than those rats or doves."

"I care now." I gazed at the ships docked and either loading or unloading supplies. The sea would never be mine again, but it had never been as important as I thought.

"Jackie?"

I gazed at her. Strands of blond hair fluttered in the wind. I'd had to buy her a new dress. This one was green with lace and ribbons around the bodice but not too tight around her still-healing belly. I knew what she wanted. An apology. Some sign that I loved her and would stay with her forever.

So I kissed her.

120

Gently, she put a hand on my chest and pushed me back. I was crushed, especially when I met her gaze and saw the sorrow there. She reached inside my sleeve and withdrew the clawed thing within. "How can I trust you?"

How, indeed? I had nothing to give her. There were no promises I could make that she would believe. My scars would never fade. I looked at the hairy, inhuman hand in hers. I didn't deserve her. Not after what I'd done. "Burn everything in the workshop and chain me to the bed." It hurt to say it. I'd spent years perfecting elixirs and herbal remedies. I didn't want to lose those recipes, but it was preferable to losing her.

"Chain you to the bed?" There was a hint of mischief in her voice. "Make you my prisoner and do devilish things to you?"

George chittered softly as she slipped a hand between my thighs and cupped me there. The hot tingling took me by surprise. I nuzzled her neck, taking in the scent of peaches. George hissed, but I ignored him. This was *my* girl, no matter what he thought.

"I want you to promise me one thing," she said.

"Anything."

"Don't fix my scars again."

I rested my paw on her belly. "Never." She was perfect as she was. We both were.

Jackie Rivera was born in Batavia to a Chinese mother and Portuguese father and speaks a half dozen languages fluently. Jackie has traveled the seas as a pirate, escaped from being a prisoner of war, studied Chinese medicine to become an alchemist and acupuncturist, and isn't afraid of a damn thing.

Traci Castleberry lives in southern Arizona with two cats and a Lipizzan mare. She's been published in numerous anthologies, is a graduate of Clarion, Taos Toolbox, and is a first reader for *The Magazine of Fantasy and Science Fiction*.

This story originally appeared in *Daughters of Frankenstein*.

CHILDREN OF THE GUILLOTINE

An essay by Bernard Asse, as provided by Nathan Crowder

You sit there smiling, full of self-importance, bloated with secrets and my finest burgundy, and question the path that brought you here to me. Our previous interactions in the Grand Salon piqued your curiosity, made you envious, perhaps. Me, the lowly child of a Parisian ex-pat and a college professor from Senegal, the talk of the city's elite, my designs worn by the daughters of wealth and privilege. You look upon my Haute Couture and see nothing special, nothing magical. Certainly, I must have done something scandalous, must have fucked my way into a position of influence, must know where the bodies are buried, to achieve such unwarranted acclaim. How tired your bleated protests, thinking they are unique, thinking you are the first to question my vision as a designer.

Rooting in the soft ground of my known history, you tried to dig up some dark secret. You found nothing but carrots but convinced yourself they were diamonds. Convinced yourself that my association with esoteric spiritualists makes me look mad, as if black magic could account for my successes.

If I truly were a sorcerer, then you were a fool to come to my home to confront me.

But we shared a laugh over it, didn't we? The blow of the accusation turning instead to an introduction, a laying bare of grievances, an opportunity to expose our true selves. To a fine meal shared between new friends.

You sit before me as the daughter of wealth and privilege, striving to make an impact in the fashion world. Too late you found that real talent cannot be bought. Your money and influence cannot bring you that spark. You cannot create, only acquire. You see yourself as less because of this. If only you knew your worth, your inherent value, perhaps you wouldn't be here.

And here I am, Bernard Asse, who came from nothing, Parisian born but raised in far off Dakar. Senegal? How can genius come from Senegal? you think. Surely this is a mistake. It illustrates your ignorance. Your lack of vision. Genius can come from anywhere. You only need be hungry for it.

My mother was hungry.

Her family was born in the blood and fire of the French Revolution, the filial ties that came before made irrelevant by the events of the time. There could be no going back. My mother's people were reborn the children of the guillotine. They learned new paths towards knowledge and power. Or perhaps old ways. Very, very old ways.

There is magic in the meat. Surely a sensualist like yourself grasps the faintest spark of that truth. But beyond the limited edge of your understanding is a universe of possibility.

The people were starving, you see. Dire circumstances such as that, it makes the previously unthinkable a reality. The suggestion of "Let them eat cake," cuts even deeper when you realize they were already at each other's throats. Ghoulish, you say? Monstrous? Those were monstrous times, my sweet. And people have to eat.

Ah. I see the horror in your eyes. I see you question the fine stew I served for dinner. You have no reason to fear. It was pork loin procured down the street. You deserve nothing finer.

Speaking of pigs, have you heard the story of the three-legged pig? Your confused expression tells me that the answer is no. But where was I?

Oh yes. Heritage.

My mother was forced to flee Paris when she was young. She had been careless, a schoolmate gone missing under mysterious circumstances. As you might expect, suspicions had been raised, and she had to leave her old life behind. Senegal had been a French territory until four years earlier, and though it was not the most welcoming place, at least it was far from curious eyes and scandalous whispers. She lived quite well there once she adjusted. Dakar is a lovely city.

124

Shame you'll never visit it, really. Paris has its charm, but there is a warmth and richness in Dakar that must be seen to be appreciated.

My parents met at university. He was a few years older, a medical student at the head of his class. He read obsessively, medical journals as well as Camus and Sartre in the original French. He spoke four languages fluently, and a smattering of at least four or five more. My father was a genius.

And my mother was hungry for knowledge.

So hungry.

They say that not everyone learns the same way. Some from reading, some from practice, some from lectures. The children of the guillotine, they consume knowledge. Nothing base. Not like you are thinking. Not like a wolf. Not like some animal gorging at the trough. There is ritual to the process. A holy communion. Beauty, even. Such beauty a mind like yours could scarcely conceive.

If you know how to see this beauty, there is magic in the meat. Knowledge, memories, secrets. Held fast in the fat and sinews, that spark can be transferred in the sacred act of consumption.

The pig. Yes, the story of the three-legged pig. I was going to tell you that story. I see the pleading in your eyes. Do not worry. I haven't forgotten.

Or are you looking for something else? Perhaps your gaze snags upon the candlelight reflecting off my cutlery? Or you hope for someone to interrupt us, perhaps? You needn't concern yourself with that. I live alone. My lifestyle requires a certain degree of discretion. Of seclusion.

Now. Where were we? Yes. The pig.

There was salesman who came upon a farm out in the countryside. In talking with the farmer, he noticed a massive hog wallowing in a pen. This magnificent beast happened to have a wooden leg. The farmer noted the salesman's curiosity and said, "I see you eying my pig. That's an amazing pig. One time I was fixing the tractor and the jack fell, pinning me under its weight. I would have died if that pig hadn't come to my rescue, pushing against the tractor enough that I could get free. A magnificent pig. Then, not too long after that, my house caught fire in the middle of the night. My family would have died had that hog's squealing not woken me up. As it was, I had enough time to rescue myself and my wife and daughter. Yes indeed, that is one amazing pig."

"But why does he have a wooden leg?" the salesman asked.

The farmer smiled and his teeth shined, sharp and cold as a guillotine. "A pig that amazing, you don't want to eat all at once."

I tell that story so that you may understand this one.

My parents met in college. They fell in love and returned to my mother's ancestral home in Paris. Where they were married. Where I was born. And over time, my brilliant, loving father wasted away before my eyes.

Well, not wasted.

Not a bite was wasted.

Whittled away, perhaps?

She loved him so much, it took years for my mother to consume him.

My mother, she was crafty. She was clever. She was subtle. Thanks to my father, she was brilliant as well.

And I, Bernard Asse, toast of the Parisian fashion scene? I was my mother's son.

I saw what she had, and I grew hungry.

I see you eying my knife. It is an heirloom. A final gift from my mother. They say the blade was forged with steel from the guillotine. I can't prove this historical footnote. But I believe it, and that's enough.

Don't bother getting up. Not that you can. Pork loin wasn't the only ingredient in the feast I served you. No, your bowl had something else in it as well. Something to help you relax.

It's not your fault. I want you to know that. Your aspirations exceeded your reach. You couldn't see your own value. So busy chasing acclaim by any means necessary that you didn't realize you had fattened yourself on other people's secrets. Secrets have currency. And for we children of the guillotine, there is magic in the meat.

I know you understand that. If not now, you will eventually.

We have time, after all.

———

Bernard Asse is a rising star in the fashion industry, known for his innovative choice of materials interpreted through a lens of classic silhouettes. He is hungry for success and his new collection will walk Milan 2020. His current whereabouts are unknown.

––––––––––

Nathan Crowder has a fondness for writing about superheroes and some of the darker corners of history and culture. He has seen every episode of *Project Runway* at least once.

FICTION

CAMOUFLAGE

By Andrew Jensen

Everybody wants something. I wanted to get off Normanderrière. That's not the real name of the planet I was born on, but it works. Everyone from my Creche calls it that, because it's the ass-end of the universe. It's only worth staying if your parents are rich enough to raise you privately, and don't farm you out to be born in a creche.

I stopped wondering if my parents might secretly be rich when I was little. Even if they *were* rich, they'd never come to save me. I couldn't rely on them. I never even learned their names. Besides, most of the adults I knew didn't want to give me anything: they just wanted pieces of *me*.

That's why I signed on as the Engineer's Assistant on the *Wombat*. Don't worry if you've never heard of her. I've changed her name. Not that it would matter. She was a small jump freighter with a small crew. I don't think she ever hauled any important cargo. That suited me fine. I just wanted to get off-planet, and I figured the captain of such a little ship might not be too worried about the rules.

I didn't have any engineering papers, but I've always been good with machines, so I lied about my tickets. For some reason, the captain didn't check my references or anything. She hired me on the spot.

I wondered what *she* really wanted. Then I met Delroy.

~

"Here you are, Del. You wanted help, now you've got it."

"Help? From a kid? How old are you, kid? Twelve?"

"I'm nineteen," I lied. I almost said twenty-one, but why push my luck?

"You know the routine. Get the kid a bunk, yada, yada." The captain started to leave. "We finish load-up in six hours and launch for a long jump in eight."

Delroy looked outraged. "What? We've barely had any leave! How am I supposed to have the ship ready that fast?"

The captain called over her shoulder, "Quit whining. Your new assistant can help you."

She went through a hatch. Just before she closed it, I heard her say to someone, "Let's see how he likes a taste of his own medicine."

Delroy looked at me funny. "Okay, kid, let's get you sorted out."

I didn't like the sound of that.

~

Delroy looked over my application. I could see it didn't fool him for a second. I wasn't sure what to do and standing there quietly was really hard. I didn't want to be put off the ship, at least until we were somewhere far away. But neither did I want the captain to use me to teach anyone a lesson. I decided I'd have to tell Delroy the truth. Sometimes, it's the only way. Then he surprised me.

"No papers, eh?" he said. "Well, we'll have to see what you can do."

He gave me a bunch of things to try and watched me closely. Most of them were pretty simple, but one or two were new to me. With those, Delroy showed me how to do it right.

"You'll do, kid. Just keep being honest with me. The captain isn't stupid. She's probably guessed, but she's made you my problem, so she won't care. Official papers aren't everything, as long as you don't do anything to screw up the ship."

What this meant, I eventually learned, is that Delroy didn't have official papers, either. Not a single ticket. But he had that old tub running perfectly. In fact, it was already prepped for a jump before the captain said anything. Thing is, he'd rigged it so the *Wombat* didn't look ready.

"Can't let the captain think she runs things," Delroy told me, grinning. "Always have one or two things with flashing yellow lights, with maybe a red thrown in for effect. Let her think you're just barely holding it together, and she won't dare treat you too bad."

"Isn't that dangerous?" I asked.

"No, no, you never mess with anything serious. That's crazy. But fiddle with minor systems? No problem. Keeps the pilots and other nosy-parkers up where they belong and away from the real systems."

The *Wombat* was Delroy's kingdom, no matter what the officers or owners thought. I have no doubt he could have been on any of those big, sleek ships that you hear about. But like he told me, once you're on one of those, you're not your own boss anymore.

I'm still not sure what Delroy wanted. To do something no one else ever did? Well, he eventually did that. To have someone admire him? No problem; he's impressed me. To find someone he could trust? That's harder. Who can you trust? I had to trust Delroy, at least not to rat me out. I don't know if he thought he could trust me.

My first real task was to load a bit of cargo for that long jump. That's not usually a job for an Engineer's Assistant, but I didn't want to complain. Then, just like he'd read my mind, Delroy explained. "It's for ship maintenance, see? The *Wombat* needs fresh paint, and the captain never keeps us in port long enough to get it done. So I have a plan. It's a long jump, so we can freshen up the paint while we're flying."

I hadn't noticed anything wrong with the paintwork I'd seen in the ship so far, but who was I to complain? So I loaded up the paint canisters and put them into a special compartment in Engineering that Delroy showed me. It was a cool design. If you didn't know where to look, you'd never know it was there.

I'm small, and I've been good at hiding for as long as I can remember. It's a great way to hear things no one wants you to hear, which can be a life-saver, and it's good for getting into places that require official documents when you don't have them. That's how I got to where the captain could hire me.

This paint storage compartment was one of the best hiding places I'd ever seen. Only one problem: if I had to use it myself, there'd be no other way out. Great cover, but nowhere to run. No

Plan B. More than good enough for paint, though. After all, paint can't run.

I'm still proud of that joke. It made Delroy laugh. No one ever laughed at my jokes before.

~

Most of the time I worked in Engineering with Delroy. Once in a while, I met other crew members in the mess, but somehow our mealtimes never quite lined up with the others. I preferred it that way, though. None of them seemed very friendly. Then again, a lot of the people I meet aren't friendly. Even the friendly-seeming ones want to get me into something messy. It's easier to keep my distance.

I did get to know most of the ship, though. Delroy took me around whenever something needed fixing. Then he'd explain what needed to be done and supervise while I did it.

I've had bosses before, back at home. A lot of them would start you working, and then wander off to talk to their friends. I never saw Delroy talk to anyone, beyond discussing the problem we were fixing. He was totally dedicated to the work. I get that. Machines are simple, and worth the time. People take a lot of effort, and never stop being unpredictable.

Like this one time I was working in a hallway. I had a cable running across, and I'd put up one of those ugly little yellow cones to warn anyone that work was going on. You'd think it would be obvious, but Delroy said I should never underestimate people's stupidity. He was right.

This crewmember came along like his head was somewhere else. He wasn't typing on a pad, or doing anything else, he was just walking. Then he tripped over what I was doing. Not the cable, like I expected, but the cone. He tripped over the warning cone!

The next thing I know he's right in my face, shouting at me. He was threatening all kinds of stuff, like putting me out an airlock. I was so terrified and furious that I couldn't answer back. It was this idiot's own fault! Why was he blaming me? What if he complained to the captain? There was nowhere to hide!

Then Delroy stepped in.

I can't remember anyone ever standing up for me before. And he was good too. I was upset, so I don't remember what Delroy said, but the crewmember turned around and hurried away without looking back.

"Don't sweat it, Kid," Delroy said with a grin. "You're *my* assistant. No one gets to tell you off but me."

It was great.

~

We almost never saw the officers. You know who I mean: the ones who never have to get their hands dirty. I'm still not sure how many there were. The *Wombat* was a small ship, so there couldn't have been more than a few.

Delroy had advice about dealing with officers too. "It doesn't pay to look too smart, or too dumb. Either one will get you noticed, and that's the last thing you want, especially if you don't have totally Kosher papers. Just keep your head down, do what you have to do, and they'll leave you alone. That way, no one interferes with any, er, independent projects you might be working on."

"Excuse me, Delroy," (I wanted to call him "Sir", out of respect, but he wouldn't let me). "When I first came aboard, I saw you arguing with the captain. Doesn't that get you noticed?"

He looked at me thoughtfully. "You're right. I can get away with that, but you can't. It'll take a while before you can suss out when it's safe and when it's not. I've got the captain figured out, so I can push it a bit. You shouldn't try it, though."

"Okay." It had never occurred to me to speak to the captain at all. Asking for the job had been bad enough. Just being on the ship was a dream come true. Why would I risk that by talking to an officer? Still, I worried.

"What if I do get noticed? What then?"

"Try to look smart enough to keep the job, but dumb enough that they won't expect any trouble from you. Don't worry, I'll show you how."

~

We were about half-way through the jump when the captain called Delroy to the bridge. I'd never been there, so I tagged along. I was curious, but I knew I had to be careful not to get noticed.

And like Delroy said, "it's better to ask forgiveness than permission." Who knew when I'd get another chance?

The bridge was disappointing. It was small, and the controls don't look anything like in the Vids. There were just three people there: the skipper and two others. Maybe a pilot and a navigator? I don't think you can navigate much in a jump. Maybe a first officer?

It's funny that I know how a ship flies, but I don't know much about flying a ship.

Coming up to the bridge was a mistake. The captain and one man glared at me, and then at Delroy. The other man was smiling. No, he was smirking. That's the word. Smirking.

"Del," said the captain, looking at a pad in her hand. "We noticed some discrepancies when we calculated our total jump mass. We're hauling quite a few more kilos than we should be. So we checked, and imagine my surprise when we found a large quantity of 'paint' hidden away in engineering. It is paint, isn't it, Del?"

"Yes ma'am," Delroy replied. He was giving the captain a winning smile. I had been copying that smile in my off time, but there was no way I'd try it now.

"So there's no chance it is, for example, a large volume of banned recreational chemicals? The kind that rots brains and brings a small fortune to smugglers?"

"No way, Cap," answered Delroy. "That stuff is nasty. I'd never have anything to do with illegal drugs."

If I'd been facing the captain, I'd have been terrified. Delroy was so calm and cool, it was obvious he had nothing to hide. Yet somehow it sounded like she was accusing him of something. And she wouldn't stop.

"Thing is, Del, there's a zero-tolerance policy for drug running. The owners are quite clear. The port authorities will seize any ship caught with drugs on board, and the owners don't want to lose their investment."

Why was she going on about drugs? The containers were all clearly labeled "paint." I checked each one.

"More to the point, none of us want to be arrested, or lose our jobs, because there's no more goddamned *Wombat* to fly. I'm sure you understand."

Delroy wasn't smiling anymore. He looked very serious. "I understand, Cap. Just in case someone switched the contents of the containers, not namin' names, of course, you want to drop the containers into jump space. Just as a precaution."

"No, Del. There are huge fines for dumping debris in the jump lanes."

"How would anyone know, Cap? When you dump in jump space, it's really hard to know where it'd come out in normal space. They couldn't track it to us." That sounded clever to me. Delroy knows his stuff. But as I started to think about it, I could see a problem. I'm not sure why Delroy didn't think of it, 'cause the captain did.

"I wouldn't want to be responsible for hitting someone with a load of drugs. Or paint, of course. What kind of a captain would I be if I allowed that?

"No, Del, you're going to use it up. The hull could use a fresh coat of paint, and you are going out there to spray every last drop. I imagine that you're pretty bored by now, so consider this a challenge."

Delroy looked like he was turning grey. "Okay, Cap. The kid and I'll—"

"No, Delroy!" The skipper looked really angry, now. "I checked over your papers. You list 'external jump work' as one of your qualifications. It's one of the reasons we signed you on. You mentioned it specifically in the interview, as I recall. You'll be doing this alone. Your assistant stays inside the ship."

For a minute there, I was really scared. I've heard stories about people going onto the hulls of ships in jump space. They say if you aren't properly trained, you start to hallucinate because of all the strange effects of the jump field. Just like SNAG and a couple of other drugs, except that you don't come out of it. You have to be prepared. Like, Kung-Fu meditation kind of prepared. Having the captain keep me on board was a relief.

Then I felt bad. I was letting Delroy down. I'm sure Delroy would have taught me well. He never screwed me over, so why should I be afraid? He was the only person who'd ever looked out for me, so I should be able to trust him, right?

Except, there's nowhere to hide on the hull of a ship in jump space. There's no escape if something goes wrong. There's no Plan B.

I was glad I didn't really have a choice.

"Go suit up now, Del. Connor here will accompany you so you don't have any problems."

I looked at Connor. He was the one who had been smirking. Now he just looked mean. He patted something on his belt. It looked like a zapper. I didn't even know there were weapons on the ship. Connor followed Delroy off the bridge.

"Shouldn't you be in Engineering?" asked the skipper, looking hard at me.

I ran.

~

Delroy didn't look happy as he left. I couldn't blame him. The captain was being mean to him, and that Connor guy looked like a bully. I felt like a traitor.

Still, I figured it should all be fine. Delroy wanted to paint. He'd said so. And he was an expert in all kinds of extreme sports and zero-G martial arts. He'd told me about those, too, in the long hours of the flight. He'd visited lots of weird places and picked up some pretty amazing skills along the way. So even if he didn't have official training for jump-work on the hull, he still had nothing to be afraid of. Besides, this would make him famous. The first man to paint a ship in mid-jump.

Except that Delroy didn't want to be famous. He talked about keeping things "on the down-low." I hadn't heard that expression before, but it made sense when I thought about it. It was like hiding: life is always better if people aren't looking at you.

~

Delroy was out painting the hull for hours. The *Wombat* isn't big, but she's a ship after all. There'd be no way to paint quickly wearing all that extra gear. I listened in on the Comm system as he reported on his progress. It didn't sound as scary as I'd imagined. It sounded awful: a boring job with everyone on the ship paying attention and crazy jump-space effects going on all around you. Maybe he made it sound boring so they would stop listening. Nobody stopped, though. I know I didn't.

When the job was finished, Delroy didn't come back in.

That caused all kinds of trouble. The captain started shouting at

Connor, and he started shouting back. I could hear other voices joining in. I shut off the Comm and curled up in a quiet corner I'd found in Engineering. Would they make me go out onto the hull to bring Delroy back in?

What would I find? I couldn't bear to think about it.

I couldn't stop thinking about it.

~

All of a sudden, we were out of jump space. Apparently, you can do that in an emergency. All it takes is a beacon to fix on. The captain pulled us out of jump right next to a military base.

I'm still not sure what happened next. One of the crew told me the sensors on the military base *Amity* couldn't detect the *Wombat* at first, and then they freaked out when they saw how close we were. Something to do with Delroy's paint job, I guess. I remember looking at the hull after we left the ship. It was weird. Like your eyes kept trying to slip off it sideways. I stopped looking right away.

What came next was no fun. We were all questioned by a series of guys in uniform. They asked me what Delroy had said about the "inherent camouflage capacity of hallucinogenic compounds applied superficially in a jump field environment." I told them he didn't say any of that. After a couple of dozen times, they finally believed me. At least, they stopped questioning me. I wasn't sure what to expect next.

Then the captain came and saw me.

~

"Hey, Kid, I know you were close to Delroy. I just want to express my sympathy."

I didn't want any fake sympathy. Especially not from the captain. But I had to behave. She knew where I came from, and she could get me sent back. I had to say something to back her off.

What I wanted to say was "you killed him! You wanted him dead!"

Actually, that might not be true. The captain seemed to be in a lot of trouble here. The Uniforms had asked me a few times if the captain had a grudge against Delroy. Like I'd tell them.

Eventually I figured it out. She was trying to teach Delroy a lesson again. Just like when she'd hired me. I still didn't tell anyone. I had to answer her. I had to pretend I hadn't figured her out. She probably didn't want anyone to know. So I played dumb.

"Sympathy, Captain? Why? It's not like Delroy's dead or anything."

"I'm afraid he must be. He lost contact with the bridge while he was painting. If he fell through the jump field bubble, he'd appear in the middle of normal space somewhere. We could never find him, even if his EVA suit could last this long."

"Did he finish painting the hull?" I'm not sure why I asked that question. It was like something had been bothering me at the back of my mind.

"Pardon?"

"Did Delroy finish the paint job? If he just came loose, there'd be part of it unpainted, wouldn't there? And the Peace Fleet sensors would have spotted us right away, 'cause of the bare patch. So he must have finished. Which means he's still alive."

I was just talking to distract the Captain, maybe thinking out loud a bit, when I suddenly realized that my words made sense! I shut up right away. I hoped she couldn't see the excitement I was feeling.

"Look, I know this is hard to accept, but he's gone. You probably blame me for—"

Don't let her know what I'm thinking! "Nah. Delroy wanted to paint the hull. That's why he brought the paint on board. He told me." Did that sound dumb enough? Would she leave me alone so I could figure out the rest?

The skipper shook her head and left the room. I didn't even get to use the next line I'd planned. *Would I be promoted if Delroy didn't come back? 'Cause, you know, that would mean extra pay, wouldn't it? Not as much as Delroy was getting, obviously, since I still had a lot to learn, but more than I was getting.* But I never got to use it. That was a relief: I didn't want to look too dumb, and I'm still not sure when I'm pushing my luck.

Turns out it would have been a really dumb question. The Peace Fleet seized the *Wombat*, and we had to hitch a ride on someone else's cargo ship. They wanted to reverse-engineer the *Wombat's* camouflage for their bigger ships.

They made us all sign something official about secrets. No problem. I've known how to keep my mouth shut for a long time. I sure wasn't going to tell them what really happened. I mean, all Delroy'd have to do to escape is paint his own suit after painting the hull. Then he'd ride on the outside until we got to a dock. Even on a military base, he could slip in unseen with that freaky paint all over him. Then he could just as easily slip aboard another ship to leave, like the one we left on. No one would ever spot him. And if anyone knows more than me about hiding, it's Delroy.

If I can figure that out, it would be easy for Delroy. Once he saw what his paint (okay, probably his drugs) were doing to the hull, he would have figured out his Plan B immediately.

I may not know much about people, but I bet that the Uniforms would never let Delroy go once they saw his invention. Even off the ship, he'd have to stay hidden. But he's too smart for them. Delroy's too smart to get caught.

He's too smart to die.

By now he's somewhere far away, with a new name. I understand that. I would have ducked out too. I still miss him, though.

That's why I'm putting his story on the Trans-Web. I want it to get through to him. I've changed all the names, of course, so they can't get me for spilling secrets. Delroy was never his real name. I probably never knew his real name.

Delroy, if you get this, maybe you could drop me a note. I'm not worried or anything. I just thought you'd like to know that someone misses you.

And, you know, if you need an assistant or anything, I'm available.

Andrew Jensen lives in Braeside, Ontario. He is the minister at Knox United Church, Nepean.

His speculative short stories have been published in over a dozen magazines and anthologies: most recently the summer issue of *Mad Scientist Journal*, as well as *Stupefying Stories*, *Dreamforge*, and *Abyss & Apex*.

Andrew is also the author of a book of Church humour called *God: The Greatest User of Capital Letters*, published by Wood Lake Books.

When not writing or ministering, Andrew plays trumpet, impersonates Kermit the Frog, and performs in musical theatre. You should have seen him as Henry Higgins ...

TELLING THE BEES

By Judith Field

Mark opened the secret desk drawer and took out the ash wood wand. The warmth from the power stored in it spread through his fingers, and he felt the wood throb like a heartbeat. He muttered an incantation, and the wand folded into two. He put in into his pocket.

Pat was in the garden. He joined her, tucking his hands deep into his pockets against the chill. "We've had a call-out," he said. "Cuddly toys manifesting in a house in Burnham."

"Give me a moment, I've got to finish this. I want these carrots to set seed for next year." Looking up at the sky, she sang a golden melody about honeysuckle and summer. The wind eased. He heard his own voice singing the chorus. The buzzing of bees filled the space. One circled his head three times before landing on his hand.

"That was its way of kissing you," Pat said. "But I'm not jealous. Bees are the world's little musicians. They love singing, and it's quicker to bribe them into the veg garden with a few verses than to grow extra flowers." She shivered. "What happened to the summer?"

"Gone." He put his arm round her and looked up at the trees, almost bare of leaves. "And where are the swallows?"

"Somewhere warm, if they've got any sense. I'm glad this job's indoors." She bent over the carrot plants. "Bye now, little musicians. I've got to go to work. And so should you." She stood up. "You've got to keep the bees up to date with everything that's going on, they easily take offence."

They returned to the house. "Animated toys," she said. "That's usually down to life force spilling over from another duality. We need to shove it back and fix the leak. Got your wand?"

He nodded and patted his jacket pocket.

"Good. Look after it. There'll be no more. Ash dieback's put paid to that."

~

The house was on a new estate, a maze of streets built between the river and the remains of Wodehouse Forest, leading nowhere. Pat and Mark picked their way along a muddy path flanked on either side by a row of terraced houses of different sizes like a mouthful of broken teeth. Each had a plot number, apparently generated at random like the lottery.

On their second pass along the street, Mark spotted Plot 16, between Plots 73 and 2. Pat knocked on the door. A man, looking about thirty, answered.

"Court and Anderson? Thank God. Come in—I'm Gerry Finch."

They stepped inside. The aromatic smell of new carpets caught in Mark's throat. Two pencil drawings hung in the hall, "Josh, Reception Class," written on each. The first one showed a beast resembling a wingless dragon, wearing a top hat and a cloak. A single black eye gazed from the middle of a face that had no mouth or nose. The second showed a cross between a dog and a rabbit, with a rat-like tail and six limbs. Its mouth, looking too large for its face, was filled with long pointed teeth.

"Josh loves to draw," Gerry said. "Teacher reckons he's got more imagination than the rest of the class put together."

He ushered them into a room at the end of the hallway. "Have a seat." Mark sat on a Chesterfield sofa covered in dazzling orange leather. Gerry perched, crossing and uncrossing his legs, on the edge of a matching, eye-watering armchair.

Pat sat beside Mark. "Gerry?"

"This is going to sound mad—"

"Not to us," Pat said. "We're used to this. Lots of entities look like toys."

144

"We'll try to find a way to sort it out," Mark said. Pat nudged him with her elbow. "I mean, we *will* sort it out. Just tell us your story."

"Moving here three months ago was meant to be a fresh start for me and Josh," Gerry said. "Our own garden and backing onto a forest. I moved a couple of fence boards. Josh likes to run round in it." He bit at a fingernail. "It was all good, till a week ago." His voice thickened and tailed off.

"It's OK, take your time," Pat said.

Gerry cleared his throat. "Those toy things showed up in Josh's room, from nowhere. Hiding under the bed." He shuddered, and a sheen of sweat appeared on his forehead. "I couldn't catch them."

"We can," Pat said.

"Hang on. Things got a whole lot worse. I heard a man's voice in Josh's bedroom late one night. Went in to tell him to turn his telly off. But it was a book."

Mark reached in his pocket and pulled out the phasmometer, a black object the size and shape of a goose egg, which detected entities. It emitted a series of staccato clicks, like dried peas dropping into a saucepan, one at a time. "A book with pictures, you press a button and it makes a sound?"

Gerry stood and paced up and down. "No, no. It was an ordinary book I got when I was a kid. *Treasure Island*. Forgot I still had it—it must be 20 years since I've looked at it. It was open on Josh's bed. He'd been drawing on the pages. The book was reading itself aloud. Stopped, when I came in."

"Can we see it?" Pat said.

Gerry shook his head. "I burnt it. Had to. It wasn't reading *Treasure Island*. It was some sort of poem, creepy weird stuff. I wasn't having Josh listen to that."

Mark leaned forward. "Can you recall the words?"

"Flowers ... blood." He shook his head. "I can't remember."

"I can." A boy aged about four stood in the open doorway.

"Go back to your room, Josh," Gerry said.

"No, Dad. Listen." He looked into the distance. A dry, creaking voice came from his mouth. "When daffodils begin to peer,
With heigh! the doxy over the dale,
Why, then comes in the sweet o' the year;
For the red blood reigns in the winter's pale,
And the sun shall flee from me in fear,

145

While I shall kill—"

Gerry grabbed his arm "Shut it. That's enough."

Josh looked at his father. "I didn't say nothing."

The clicks from the phasmometer changed from single peas to a harvest. Mark showed it to Pat. "Ever seen a count rate like this?"

Her eyes opened wide. "Some massive, unstable source of power is near, and coming closer. Getting stronger." She stood. "I don't think it was Josh saying that."

Gerry let go of Josh's arm and slumped onto the sofa "What are you on about? We all saw him." He held his head in his hands. "This is doing my nut in. Just go, Josh."

Josh ran from the room. His footsteps thudded along the hallway. A door slammed.

"We need to talk to him," Pat said.

~

Pat sat next to Josh on the bed. His chin rested on the drawing pad he clutched to his chest.

Mark heard a scuffling sound.

"Look out," Josh said, curling his legs under himself, as the dog-rabbit from the drawing in the hall shot its head out from under the bed frame, nipped Pat on the ankle, and pulled its head back. "Too slow."

"Ouch!" Pat said. "See if you can flush them out, Mark. Then we'll zap them."

Mark crouched by the bed and poked underneath it with his ash wand. He felt something roll away from him and edged his hand into the gap. The tips of his fingers chilled as they closed round the object.

Pat put her arm round Josh. "It's not a very nice toy, is it?"

His face reddened and his lower lip wobbled. "The other one's mean too. They won't let me sleep. Dad's cross all the time. It's my fault."

Pat's voice softened. "Of course it's not. But where'd they come from?"

"They just come. When I draw with Woodface's pencil."

Pat reached out for the drawing book. "Can I see?"

Josh handed it to her. She flicked through the pages, all blank.

"Can't draw any more. Lost my pencil," Josh said.

146

Mark stood up, holding what he had found under the bed. It looked like bundle of twigs held together with a pencil lead in the centre. He felt the throb of a pulse deep inside it.

"Mine," Josh shouted. "Not yours. Gimme."

Pat recoiled. "That reeks of dark magic. We need to take it away with us. Start a binding ritual to immobilise it, Mark." She turned to Josh. "Who's Woodface—your teacher? Where did he get it?"

"Woodface lives in the forest. I didn't steal it. I found it lying by our fence. He said I could have it."

The pencil writhed like a snake, driving a splinter into Mark's palm. He jerked his hand and the pencil fell to the floor. Josh grabbed it and ran.

They dashed after him, into the kitchen. Gerry looked up from his seat at the table.

"He's in the garden."

Through the kitchen window, Mark caught a glimpse of Josh stepping through the gap in the fence, into Wodehouse forest. He flung the back door open, and they rushed out. Turning sideways, Mark followed Josh through the gap, pulling Pat after himself.

"Wait, I'm coming too," Gerry called. He rushed at the fence and stretched a hand toward it. With a crack, a massive spark jumped across the gap. Gerry jerked his hand back.

The smell of singed hair tickled Mark's nostrils. He pulled out his wand and used it to draw the shape of a door in the gap between the panels.

Gerry extended one of his feet. He wrenched it back again. "I can't get through. What is it—electric?"

"Worse than that. No time to explain," Pat said. "You'll have to stay here. We'll find Josh."

~

Pat gripped Mark's hand. A muddy path wound between the trees, through a dense carpet of dull green leaves with saw-like edges. Mark called Josh's name. No reply. Nettles towered over them on both sides. Damp air seemed to cling to the stalks. Ragged leaves hung down, patched with white as though splattered with dirty water.

Mark remembered a legend in a grimoire of Pat's, a tale of things in the woods, which blended among the trees without being seen. In the legend, you could hear muttering in the breeze, trees whispering to each other.

They reached a clearing, dotted with builders' rubble. In each corner stood an ash tree, bark flaking. The few remaining leaves were withered and blotched with black. Between the trees, a blue-green net of power flickered on and off like a faulty lamp.

"Someone planted those trees," Pat said, "so that the pattern in the lines of force coming from them would keep something trapped inside. But the trees are dying and the power's failing. Something hideous has broken free."

On the far side of the clearing stood the remains of a stone archway. As they drew closer, Mark saw that the stones that had formed its sides were carved with images of smiling, winged women with six arms, flanked by flowers. Below the waist, their insect-like bodies tapered to pointed tails.

"Nobody's done anything like this for hundreds of years," Pat said, "but it used to be standard practice to lock evil into the keystone, the centre of an arch, with carved goddesses standing guard."

"It might have stood there forever. Nobody would have known, if the builders hadn't cleared the space," Mark said.

Pat nodded. "The ash trees, now they're something I've only read about. They'd be a back-up, in case the arch fell. A back-up that failed. And Josh found his way in. Over there."

Josh sat on one of the fallen stones, drawing. They crept toward him. He looked up. "I've nearly finished copying this picture of Woodface. He's there, on the ground." He pointed at the larger, wedge-shaped keystone, carved with stylised leaves, smoothed by time.

Mark looked at Josh's drawing of the leaves. At first as blurred as the ones on the stone, they grew sharper, shimmered, and regrouped into a face. The face of a man, with hair and beard made of leaves. Shoots grew out of the nostrils and open mouth.

"That's his head," Josh said. "I'm just finishing his body." The pencil scudded across the page, drawing something tall and broad, with legs like tree trunks. "All done!"

The air filled with the sound of whispering. Ivy growing on a tree rippled and turned, but there was no wind. A fern frond broke from its root with a sharp snap and writhed toward the edge of the clearing.

Mark's pulse and breathing quickened. He pulled Josh to his feet. The pencil and book fell to the ground.

A shape, man-like but rough-carved from lumps of wood, lumbered into the clearing, crackling as it came. It stopped an arm's length from them, its leaf-face scabbed with fungus.

"Not Woodface. Woodwose," Pat gasped. "Wodehouse. Woodwose. I should have known—this place breathes evil."

Mark pulled his wand out and jabbed it forward. He flung it away as it burst into flames, burning to fine powder.

The woodwose opened its mouth in a grin, showing teeth made of jagged stumps of rotting wood. "Ash to ashes," it said, in a voice like twigs scraping across stone. "Fetters of stone and ash can no longer hold me." It raised an arm and pointed a hand knotted like a bundle of dried roots at Mark. "Be a tree."

Mark's limbs stiffened and locked. He felt a thrill like an electric shock running up from the earth as it rose around his feet. "Pa-at." His voice was slow and mechanical, like an old-fashioned vinyl record played at the wrong speed "Bind-ing ..."

Pat began reciting the ritual.

The woodwose raised a club-like arm and staggered toward her. Her voice faded. "Your words have no hold over me," it said. "My power is empathic. It thrives on feelings. On the fear of woman and man." It pushed her to the ground. Her ankle bent underneath her as she fell. The woodwose moved toward Josh.

With unfocussed eyes, Josh took a pace forward.

Mark tried to cry out. His jaw locked, choking the sound into a murmur.

The woodwose turned and smashed its arm into Mark's face. "Silence. A tree has no voice."

Blood dripped from Mark's nose. Clear, like sap. The woodwose turned toward Josh. "I have consumed summer. Earth will know it no more. The child awoke me. I thirst for his essence. Come."

Tree root fingers clutched Josh around the throat. His knees buckled, and he collapsed to the ground, eyes closed. A shimmering mist snaked out of his nostrils and mouth. The woodwose bent over him.

"You can't have him!" Pat dragged herself across the ground and clutched Josh's hand.

"I will devour you too, woman. But first, the boy. Younger. Sweeter." It bent lower, burying its face in the mist.

Pat dropped Josh's hand and hauled herself to her knees. Gasping, as she picked up one of the fallen stones from the arch. Her arms shook as she lifted it and her fingers opened. It fell into a patch of mud, the winged goddess carved on it smiling up at the sky. Wings. Body like an insect. Mark willed his lips to open. He forced out a croak. "Tell ... the bees."

Pat scooped up the ash from the burnt wand and held it in her cupped hands. She hobbled to her feet. "Wodewose. Hear me." The echo of her voice cracked around the clearing. The wodewose looked up. "Your empathic magic cares about feelings. But I use literal magic. And that cares about what you do." She flung the ash into its face. It howled, holding its head in its hands. Pat turned her face to the sky and sang "Honey bees, honey bees, hear what I say. An evil has taken the sun away. And now I beg you freely stay. And gather honey for many a day. Bonny bees, bonny bees, save us this day." She stared upward. The woodwose lurched toward her.

Mark felt a stirring strength in the empty sky. A swirling, buzzing shadow appeared above them. The sound grew, as the swirl solidified into bees. More and more came, until the air was filled with the sound. The swarm covered the woodwose. It howled and keened as it hobbled in circles, beating at the bees with gnarled fists.

The buzzing grew louder. Mark heard noise inside his head, whining at a higher and higher pitch until his eyes watered and his ears rang. With a bang, like a car backfiring, the woodwose exploded into a mass of swirling dead leaves. Mark felt the stiffness in his muscles dissolve. He lifted a hand and rubbed his eyes.

Josh lay, surrounded by dead and dying bees, the mist gone from his face. Pat knelt by his side. "It's over, Josh. You're OK." No movement came. Pat touched his forehead. "He's cold. So cold."

With a cry, Gerry burst into the clearing. "What happened?" He pulled Pat away. He laid his head on Josh's chest. "What's wrong with him? Wake up, lad."

"I'm sorry. We were too late," Pat said.

"For what?" Gerry stood up, his lips curled into a snarl. "You and your mumbo jumbo. What have you done?"

Mark dragged his feet out of the earth that had engulfed them.

He staggered toward Josh, singing the last line of the incantation. All he knew would have to be enough. "Save us this day."

The clouds parted, letting through a faint beam of sunlight. A bee rose from among its dead sisters. It flew toward Josh. Gerry went to swat it away. Mark grabbed his hand. "Let it come." The bee flew in a shaky circle around Josh's head three times, before landing on his nose. Josh sneezed. He opened his eyes.

Judith lives in London. She is the daughter of writers, and learned how to agonise over fiction submissions at her mother's (and father's) knee. In 2009, she made a New Year resolution to start writing fiction and get published within the year. Pretty soon she realised how unrealistic that was but, in fact, it sort of worked: she got a slot to write a weekly column in a local paper shortly before Christmas 2009. It ran for a several years. She still writes occasional feature articles for the paper.

Her fiction, mainly speculative, has appeared in a variety of publications, in the USA, UK Australia and New Zealand. She is Science Fiction Editor at *Red Sun Magazine*.

This story originally appeared in *The Book of Judith*.

A NATURAL HISTORY OF
HEADLESS SOCIETY

By Valerie Lute

By March, faithful reader, I found myself in the Land With No Heads. As you know by now, I had felt lost and loveless since the day I returned from overseas to find Ashley had abandoned our apartments, but I did my best to throw myself into my new ethnography. There was only one road in this country, thereby reducing my sense of aimlessness.

As I traversed the wide and white path, I passed the headless bodies of the natives. They shambled along, the gray stiff skin on their legs crackling with each movement. Some were nude, with lumpy genitalia hanging in the wind. Others wore suits or simple dresses. They bowed to me, and I would repeat the gesture. If I've learned one thing in my travels, it is how to blend into a culture, even with a strong head on my shoulders.

I never saw the sun in this land. The grass grew tall, but was as white as the dusty road. After several days of walking the path and sleeping on a hard bed of earth, my back ached terribly. I grew older with each year, and with each lost love. But at last, I reached the temple.

I heard many tales of this temple during my expeditions on the Ionian Sea, and despite sailor's propensity toward hyperbole, none exaggerated the temple's size. It was like a marble mountain dropped in the middle of plains and carved into smooth pillars and archways. This was a temple without gold, without icons and without gods. Red-winged blackbirds nested in the corners, making the only adornments.

Devotees flitted in and out of the temple in the way I had seen out east. Headless monks bowed to each visitor they passed. Headless men in peasant rags slept underneath the arches. Headless mothers pressed babes to their ashen breast. The babes had small crying faces still intact, not yet having reached coming of age. According to rumor, in a ceremony at seven years, the children undergo a rite of either magic or mad science wherein they survive decapitation and go on to walk and behave almost as full men. To my knowledge, no foreigner has observed the ritual first-hand, at least none who have returned.

Three monks swarmed me in the temple entrance. How they sensed me, I know not. They gestured with their hands to indicate a sphere above their stumpy necks and pressed into me, closer and closer, until I could smell the sweat soaked into their habits.

"I'm a friend," I managed to say just before a fourth monk appeared, offering a plate of green grapes.

As I've learned in my travels, when someone offers you food, you accept it. The grapes were sweeter than I expected, though they featured a thick seed. The other monks backed away as I ate, and soon the monk with the grapes also walked, gesturing for me to follow.

The temple had open, almost Grecian architecture. The outer portion consisted of a wide and pillared veranda, and the inner rooms were set off by doorless arches that ingeniously allowed light to bounce down the white walls even as we delved deeper into the building.

The monk and I entered a room overwhelmed by a slab altar. A man knelt before it on a straw mat. To my surprise, this adult still had a head. When he looked over his shoulder at me, I saw it was quite a good head at that. He had the sort of face women love to kiss, with childish lips and heavy-lidded eyes. He bowed before the altar once more before he rose to greet me.

"Were you praying?" I asked.

"Where do you think you are?" he grinned. "You're not a pilgrim, I take it."

"No," I said. "I'm just a visitor."

He pouted in disappointment. "I'm Ricary," he said, clasping my hand. "And this is Vesheda." He nodded toward the headless monk who escorted me.

"I didn't realize he had a name," I said.

"Of course," Ricary replied. "You don't need a head to have an identity." He untied the top of Vesheda's robe, and there was the name tattooed in stretched letters across his anemic chest.

"Well, visitor," Ricary went on, "I suppose you want to see what we do here." He pressed his palm on my shoulder and ushered me out of the room.

He kept talking as we walked down the corridor. "I was once a traveler like you, yes," he said. "Sailed the *septem maria*, drove camels though the ad-Dhana Desert, even nearly died of dengue fever navigating the Ganges. I only came here because I did not believe. But now I see that not believing is everything."

"And you became a novice here?" I asked. "Even as a foreigner?"

He nodded. "Six months I've been preparing. Before, my life was tormented by emotions and senses, love and loss. Now I'm ready to devote myself to life's true meaning."

At his mention of love and loss, I thought again of finding Ashley gone, the dustless square of floor before our bed, the space where the wedding chest used to sit. The white chambers we passed through were much the same—space begging to be left unfilled.

We entered a kitchen where headless monks were preparing a meal. One stoked a fire, another stirred a pot. A young monk chopping vegetables cut a chunk out of his thumb. He bled on to the beets.

"Newly initiated," Ricary whispered shyly. Then he turned into the host again. "You can see here how we do good deeds. We prepare food for all our pilgrims."

We walked through the kitchen and into the dining room. Here headless devotees threw salad in the air. They poured soup on their necks and rubbed it into their flesh.

"All the food we serve here is pure," Ricary said. "Straight from our own garden. We don't even wash off the dirt."

I couldn't help but stifle a laugh. Ricary, resembling a wounded bird, drew himself eye to eye with me. He did not need to further reprehend me—that look alone was unbearable.

"Sometimes I forget that I too once laughed," he said, speaking sympathetically but retaining his sad countenance. He reached out and brushed my eyelids with his fingers. "But I hope to one day be a wiser man, without the lies of these."

"My apologizes," I said. "I meant no offense."

"You never need to say you are sorry," he answered. "You only need to agree."

I wondered about the source of this reasoning, but before I could inquire, he resumed his stream of speech, saying, "Now I must attend my first initiation ritual. You're welcome to observe."

He never stopped talking on our way down the hall. He rolled up his sleeves and showed me his scars. "This one," he said, tracing a line down his forearm, "I got from a duel I nearly lost. And this," he showed a jagged star on his elbow, "is from falling out of a tree when I was nine. Never stopped me from climbing a tree or mast or anything else."

I found it odd that a man so vibrant would choose to be cloistered in a plain and silent monastery. Although lacking a conversation partner for six months may have prompted his verbosity, his childish mannerism revealed a man who needed people too much, who based his happiness on the reactions of others. Novice monks with such qualities never make it.

He asked me then if I were lucky enough to be scarred, but we reached the room before I could answer.

Here a monk lay out metal rods that I knew well from my years traveling with sailors.

"He is a true master," Ricary said as he stripped off his robe, "to do this without sight." He lay down on a mat. With one hand the master pulled Ricary's skin tight, and he began the tattoo.

Knowing that this might take hours, I asked if I might have a seat.

"Make yourself at home," Ricary said, smiling through a wince of pain.

I sat against the wall with the marble floor killing my old back, and watched the black line begin to grow on Ricary's muscles. I saw tears well in his eyes, and noticed his fists were rolled into tight balls. This, I knew, was wrong. I reached over, took his hand and spread the palm flat. Ricary's arm went limp, and he began to breathe easier. He turned to me and offered a nod of thanks.

After a few minutes, I set his hand back on the ground. I watched the tattooing for a while but soon fell asleep. When I awoke, the sun had long since set. The headless monks had no use for candles, but moonlight still reached our room. After my eyes adjusted to the darkness, I saw black letters stood bold on Ricary's skin. The master painstakingly perfected the curve of the final letter. Ricary's eyes were wet but happy when he looked my way. He lay still while the master gathered his tools and left the room. After a few minutes, he sat up and wrapped his robe around his shoulders.

"I'll show you to bed now," he said.

Though I was no longer tired, I didn't question it.

~

We shared quarters that night, speaking in hushed voices of our world travels. He was born in the same county as I, though he nearly twenty years later. In his day, as in mine, it was nothing but sheep and verdant lea with no neighbors for miles and no towns beyond scattered dirt-road hamlets. While the lonesomeness sparked my curiosity about other societies, for him the dullness drove his search for adventure. But any man or woman only has so many years of travel before the emptiness begins.

As we lay in bed at sunrise, Ricary's fingers crept toward the letters on his chest. I peeled his hand away and held it in mine.

"I know I can't touch it yet," Ricary said, "but it is so exciting." In the early morning light, his eyes were aglow in wonderment, like a child seeing the ocean for the first time. I couldn't help but embrace him.

Reader, I have traveled all over the globe, and I must confess: this was not my first intimacy with a monk. Morning gongs were being sounded, loud enough to send vibrations through the floor for even the dumbed monks to feel.

"I won't cause you trouble, will I?" I asked.

"There is no trouble here," Ricary said, stroking my neck with his finger. "I want so badly for you to understand."

He showed his scars again. "Touch these."

I ran my finger along the line, then leaned to embrace him, but he pulled away.

"No, no, no," he said. Gongs rang again, and he rose from the bed.

He took me to the dining room and served me porridge with the headless pilgrims. The food was surprisingly good, and I found it a shame that the headless ones did nothing but splatter it on their bodies.

Ricary told me that he would not accompany me that morning. "Sometimes people learn better on their own," he said, somewhat sad.

It hurt my heart when Ricary's smile was gone even for an instant. Then Ricary himself was gone, and the headless men slapping porridge on their skin no longer felt funny, but instead acutely depressing.

I've loved more people than I could count in more countries than I could name, but I felt Ricary had some ineffable magic. Though, as I am sure you know, it always seems that way in the beginning. I did not entertain the idea that we could run off together—Ricary's excitement for his new religion was legitimate, even if I doubted his commitment—but I considered how long I might prolong my stay. If a man like Ricary could find meaning in this place, there might yet be hope for even an old skeptic like myself.

After I finished breakfast, I wandered into the corridor. As I was alone in the temple for the first time, I noticed a dim reflection in the polished walls. I could regard my appearance for the first time since I visited my deserted home. My jowl had grown heavier, as it did with every new year and every new country, transforming my head into globule indistinguishable from my neck.

I closed my eyes and felt the creases in my face. My hands read the tale of a soul who traveled far and found nothing. But perhaps nothingness had a truth too. After all, this temple was dedicated to nothing, but in it, someone made me feel love.

I considered observing the habits of the monks for the remainder of the day but then conjectured that if personal meditation is the primary practice of this faith, perhaps I should experiment myself. I found an altar-room and knelt as I had seen Ricary doing when we met. I gripped my arms, feeling where sun and wind had blessed my skin with history. I was still kneeling when Ricary found me for dinner.

~

When we were alone that afternoon, I told Ricary how I was beginning to feel. "I understand what my hands are telling me," I said. "They show what I have lost and gained. There is something

158

heartbreaking beautiful in taking ownership of my own history. As if I am in control of my dreams and destiny."

"Oh, my sweet visitor," Ricary said with an exasperated sigh. "Your hands can't lie to your head, but your head can and will lie to your hands. Dreams, beliefs, beauty—all these falsehoods begin within your skull."

"I'm not sure I follow," I said.

"Sometimes I forget how much I learned since I came here. You've made progress today." He patted my hair.

Unanswered questions pierced like a barb in my gut. Abandoning beliefs, I could understand. As a cultural scientist, I've found that no society's beliefs are more true than another's. But dreams, beauty? Weren't these the things that made life worth living? Or was that in itself a belief?

Ricary took my hands in his. He ran his fingers over the lines and calluses that time had left there.

"Yes," he said after a careful study, "I can imagine many lies your head might tell you about these hands." He pressed my hand to his cheek. "But you can unlearn all that. Just stay with me."

I had a sudden vision of my hand being held before a gray stump neck, twisted and gnarled as a dead branch. I jerked my hand away.

"Your head," I asked, "will you cut it off?"

Ricary laughed. "We do it carefully. You sound so frightened."

Though I considered myself a tolerant soul, I admit I searched Ricary's bright eyes for signs of fear, or any other emotion I knew as human. He only smiled his same smile.

Noises erupted from another part of the temple. I was so accustomed to the silent natives, that it took me a minute to recognize it as shouting. The gongs began.

Only now did Ricary hold palpable terror in his eyes.

"Stay here," he said and ran from the room.

In the name of research, I followed him, from a safe distance. Monks rustled toward the vibrations, blindly knocking into me if I didn't move out of their way.

The shouts were coming from the front veranda. I could discern chants of "I believe, therefore I am," and "Great gods give great heads." When I passed the front archway, I saw men and women with the gray bodies of the headless ones, but they had children's heads sewn onto their necks with garish colored thread.

They must have dug up heads from those who have come of age. The heads often did not match the body's sex and looked minuscule strapped on an adult's body. In all, there must have been a score of them.

The monks tried to push the invaders out of the temple, but in their blindness, they more often than not fought each other instead. The invaders had snatched an infant away from its headless mother. She reached out for it, slowly and vainly combing the air.

Ricary, with his sight, led the charge. "Blasphemers," he yelled and knocked one to the ground, a hulking broad-chested man with the face of an apple-cheeked girl. Ricary leapt upon him, trying to twist the sewn-on head from his body.

The prettiness of Ricary's face was distorted by hatred. The other invaders tried to tear Ricary from their compatriot, but he shook them off like a mad dog. His victim sobbed as the threads snapped one by one, until at last the head popped off.

Ricary threw the head out of the temple, and the remaining invaders chased after it, continuing their chants, while the decapitated man crawled out on his own. During the scuffle, one of them had already escaped with the infant. The mother's arms still searched, and the monks persisted in fighting amongst themselves.

Ricary swung around, still full of anger and bile, and saw me lingering behind the archway. "You don't understand," he said in a pleading voice that didn't match his choleric expression.

I walked toward him slowly, holding my hands up in surrender, knowing it takes a careful anthropologist to navigate religious conflicts.

"Ricary," I asked in my most amicable voice, "who were those people."

He lumbered toward me. His body language had altered so much, he seemed a different person than yesterday. His strong shoulders hung low at his sides, and his eyes refused all contact with mine. "Dissenters," he muttered.

"I'm sorry your peace was disturbed," I said. "Do you know what they want?"

He finished bridging the distance between us. "To destroy our traditions. They steal our children so they can't undergo coming of age. You've already heard too much, I'm sure."

"Is everyone safe for now?" I said.

His breaths were still heavy and frightful. "You," he said. "You're not safe."

"Calm down," I said. "How am I not safe?"

"You are infected," he said, tilting his face up for the first time. "You heard their ideas. Now you are infected."

His eyes were delirious. I took a step back. He grabbed my arms.

"I wanted you to have a choice," he said. "but I can't let you choose wrong."

I tried to wrench myself away, but Ricary only tightened his grip. He was younger than me and still in the apex of his strength.

The sudden violence made me forget my scientific training. "You don't treat someone you love this way," I shouted.

"Love?" Ricary almost laughed. "Love is only a sickness of the head. But soon you'll learn." His voice has a smooth and calming quality even as he dragged me farther inside, into corners of the temple I hadn't yet seen.

The high arched corridors gave way to narrow tunnels. The walls grayed as the light faded. Soon we were in total darkness. We must have reached the center of the marble monolith. I stopped struggling. Even if I could escape, I was lost, and Ricary, who seemed to know these halls by instinct, could surely recapture me.

I felt Ricary use his body to push aside a door. The room that opened before us was lit by a central fire, and the cavernous walls were stained with smoke. Through an aperture above the fire, I could see a spray of clouds.

A sort of modified stocks sat beside the fire pit. It was black iron with feet that clawed into the floor. The top, where the victim's neck would rest, had a wide slit that extended down the sides. Nearby, the hilt of a short sword jutted from the fire pit. I could infer the rest.

Here Ricary was at a loss. Typically men were locked inside the stocks willingly. It was only intended to prevent those involuntary movements from interfering with the ritual. Ricary had no way to hold me while he opened the stocks. There wasn't a rope or chain in the room.

When Ricary released me to open the stocks, I stepped around him and grabbed the sword from the fire. He made a go as if to tackle me, and it was all I could muster to hold the sword steady in front of me, as if brandishing a sheath.

"I'm trying to help you," he said.

"I like my head," I replied. "We're rather attached."

We stared each other down. He was waiting for me to blink. Without warning, he kicked my shin. When I leapt away from the blow, he grabbed my sword hand.

"There is nothing to be afraid of," he said. "I'll show you."

With my hand still grabbing the sword, he pulled the blade up to his neck, and with one swift yank, cleaved his head from his neck.

To this day, I swear that when the steel touched him, Ricary's eyes lit up like lanterns, though it could have been the reflection of the glowing hot blade. Not one drop of blood was spilled. The head simply slid to the floor, its smile only disturbed by the bump as it hit the ground. The body followed its instinct to inspect the new stump, prodding and poking it with its hands.

I immediately scooped the head off the floor. It blinked slowly and said, "Hello, my visitor." The eyes had no expression. It was like a ceramic replica of Ricary's head, bloodless and glazed white. And I knew that the man dear to me was dead, even if this thing spoke with his voice.

"Can you get us out of here?" I asked it.

"I can try, but I knew it by my feet. Currently, I'm just the idea man." Its eyes pointed toward the lurching body. "He knows but doesn't say. I say but don't know. Isn't that Lao Tzu?" He chuckled.

I tried to pull the body out into the hall to get it going, but it stubbornly refused to move. Totally self-involved, it stroked the scars on its arms.

"Ah, he'll move when he's hungry," the head said. "Myself, I am thankfully free of what Joseph Addison called the most violent appetites—lust to perpetuate oneself and hunger to preserve oneself. Now my only appetite will be what the poets call the hunger for a great idea."

After some painful minutes, while the head continued quotations, the body began to wander down the hall. I followed, holding on to the hem of its sleeve with one hand and carrying the head, who had begun reciting Voltaire, in my other.

When we were in the darkest part of the corridors, the head grew quiet for a moment. After some thought, it said, "I suppose you'll be leaving once we get out of here."

162

"Of course," I said rather harshly. Then I reneged. "You know, I could bring you both to my biologist friends. Perhaps they can—"

"His home is here," the head interrupted. "As for myself, I know not. If home is where the heart is, can a head have a home? Let me ask you this my friend, where is your next ethnography?"

I felt reluctant to tell, as I had no desire for such an insufferable creature to accompany me. But then I answered, "I heard there is a tribe in the south that survives without their hearts."

After all, reader, no one deserves to be alone. Or at least, so I believe. I readjusted my grip on the head and walked straight toward the light.

———

Valerie Lute is a writer whose short stories are forthcoming or have appeared in *Arts & Letters*, *Literary Orphans*, and *Contrary Magazine*, among others. She teaches Writing the Strange at the Cambridge Center for Adult Education.

RESOURCES

SCENES AROUND THE LAB
By Lady C. Zytal, as provided by Lucinda Gunnin

Greetings Chickadees,

It's been a long, hot summer in Philadelphia. And did I mention, hot?

The International Association of Mad Scientists and Madder Engineers has agreed to change its name to maddest scientists and engineers because they're damn sick of people ignoring everything they say and then expecting them to fix it. With record-breaking heat in many parts of the world, IAMSME will refrain from saying "I told you so" if people would actually start taking action to do something about it. Since they won't, IAMSME is MADDEST and ready to start the revolution.

IAMSME operatives were busy in July in Puerto Rico, working with the local population to start putting things right, and that meant evicting the Union of Insane Politicians' idiot-in-charge there. With the success of this first test of their revolution hypothesis, the teams are ready to move to the mainland. They tell me that you can pick up your guide to ousting fascist executives at iamsme.org/overthrowtheorange

In Puerto Rico, about half a million people, or 13% of the population, came together in San Juan to protest the UIP executive who needed removal. Generally speaking, the experts say you don't need that large a percentage of the population to have a successful revolution. According to James DeFronzo (*Revolutions and Revolutionary Movements*, James DeFronzo, Fourth Edition, 2011, Westview Press), you need five major conditions for a successful revolution:

- Mass frustration leading to local uprisings;
- Dissident elites;
- Powerful unifying motivations;
- A severe crisis paralyzing state administration and coercive power; and
- A permissive or tolerant world context.

While I understand that he's the expert, I believe you also need an executive with some ability to feel shame for his actions. Because of his membership in the UIP and his mistaken belief that Article 2 of the Constitution gives him unlimited power, the orange one may require a larger percentage of the population willing to rise up to remove him. Additionally, it's unlikely a Hurricane Maria is going to hit the mainland and unify the populace.

So, dear chickadees, if you want to see IAMSME go back to being just mad and madder, it's time to Rise Up. You can make a difference and be saying the words Madam President in just 18 short months. Sooner, if we can take out the whole orange crew.

~

Maddest Scientist Allegra Mascaro introduced the world to her newest mind control device on the Fourth of July holiday. Allegra said she had just about enough of people disrespecting their neighbors, folks with PTSD, and the animal kingdom with loud explosions to celebrate a holiday filled with jingoism.

To address the issue, Allegra created Fantasta Bombs and marketed them as the best fireworks ever. Of course, consumers never read the fine print. If they had, they would have seen that the bombs are filled with a patented micro-organism that permeates the air in a half-mile radius around the bomb's explosion. The micro-organism implants in the human ear and burrows its way into the brain.

There, it makes the person believe that the first bomb was a dud that did nothing but smoke and that all subsequent bombs are the most brilliant fireworks displays that the individual has ever seen. The hallucinations caused by the micro-organism are both auditory and visual and usually last for an hour after initial exposure. The organism then dies, causing no permanent damage to the person and no disturbance of others nearby.

Or at least that was what it was supposed to do. Unfortunately, the human trials conducted in the lab did not properly mimic actual usage. In reality, in many areas, including this reporter's Main Line neighborhood, people were exposed to the organisms repeatedly by neighbors on all sides and often subjected to multiple exposures simultaneously. The overdose of micro-organisms caused severe hallucinations, some causing pain or mental distress, and often lasting for several days.

Allegra said she also did not consider the implications of consumers' desire to have fireworks for multiple days leading up to the holiday and afterwards. "We based all our data on single exposures, maybe twice a year for those areas that do fireworks for New Year's Eve as well," she said.

While the increased hospital visits and fireworks-related injuries have not officially been tied to Fantasta Bomb, Allegra announced August 1 that she was pulling them from the market. "We assumed people would be so satisfied with our product that they wouldn't try to use others while under its effects. Sadly, we underestimated the percentage of the population that will blow up anything they can get their hands on, including their hands."

Allegra categorically denies any problems with the product itself, saying the fault lies in consumers. "I'd seen the idiot label warnings for years and just assumed that was some marketing guy being overly funny and cautious. Turns out, people really are that dumb."

~

Now, on to happier matters, like my love life. After reading about her namesake and the incident in the garden, Amelia called me. I was traveling to the near past, trying to convince some people that they should have done things differently in 2016, so it took me a few days to get her message, but when I did, she asked me out to dinner.

We had a lovely night at the Brazilian steakhouse in King of Prussia and I only got a little caught up in how the city got its very unusual name. I got a bit tipsy on their very generous pours of sugar cane whiskey—like a stronger version of rum—and waxed eloquently about the inn that gave the city its name. "Welsh Quakers did it" seems like a good explanation to me!

Of course, some blame Ben Franklin and his satirical essay "An edict by the King of Prussia," but I prefer to credit the inn. The inn remained preserved in its original location until 2000, when it was moved to make way for progress in the area. It is not, as some people might have said, part of the King of Prussia mall, a structure that as of 2019 is the largest indoor shopping mall in the United States.

I may have rambled a great deal in my nervous condition.

Anyway, Amelia saw me safely home to the *Americana* and professed her undying love, or maybe I told her I love her. It's difficult to recall exactly what happened.

Not quite trusting that it's me and not my time machine she loves, we've decided to take it slow this time around. I also need to be certain our reunion was not just fueled by steak and alcohol.

Wish me luck, dear readers.

Ilsa Braun Frankenstein has become something of a bestie now that she resides in my Caribbean lair, so we spent many days dissecting my entire conversation with Amelia. Ilsa has come to the conclusion that we should be shopping for wedding dresses. So I'm asking for hints, my dears. If we get to that point, where (and when) is the best place to shop for wedding dresses? Classic or modern? Ilsa's a dear, but her dress had glowing lights, and I don't think that's me at all.

The other person paying far too much attention to my love life is Princess Tartan. After her father, King Malcolm of Juno, decided that Americans had to learn to live with the error of their ways, the Princess was heartbroken. She'd been looking forward to eating a boatload of corrupt politicians.

Since eating her way out of her depression was expressly forbidden, she's devoted herself to hopepunk. She has an Etsy store where she sells handicrafts, Junoian love potions, and antifascist materials. Princess Tartan says that she is more svelte than ever before and has just the outfit to wear should I get married. And she wants to go along when I go dress shopping. I guess it's better that she likes me and isn't interested in me as a snack, right?

She has assured me that once the UIP has been properly ousted from authority, her father will remove his restrictions on her dietary habits, and she'll get on with eating corrupt politicians. She's asked me to poll my readers to determine who would taste the best, reminding them that fatty meat often has the best flavor. She's also asked that readers create a menu for her, including which politicians to eat as appetizers, main course, and dessert. She's limiting herself to three a day in hopes of maintaining the weight loss that came with her parent-imposed diet.

The Princess has encouraged me to get married before the UIP loses power so that she can look appropriately stunning at the event. She insists that although she has complete control of her appearance when in a congealed form, she prefers to be honest about her body shape and size.

~

And with that, dear ones, I must bid you adieu. I need to retreat to Canada for a break from these end of summer temperatures and to find a little solitude to determine where Amelia and I go from here.

Love and stuff,
Lady C.

———

Lady C. Zytal was born just off the Main Line in Pennsylvania when such a thing still mattered, the first daughter of a family whom she prefers not to name. She makes her home aboard the airship *Americana*, when not at her summer lair in the Canadian Rockies or wintering on a private island near the Bahamas. Zytal considers Liz Smith her most apt pupil and the best mentor she ever had. She's also been known to denigrate simpleton scientists whose creativity ends at a bloody lab coat and death ray.

———

Lucinda Gunnin is a short story author and commercial property manager in the western Philly suburbs, a few miles past the end of the Main Line. Her collection of horror short stories *Seasons of Horror* is available online and her story "Righteous Anger" was included in *Fitting In: Historical Accounts of Paranormal Subcultures*. Her flash story "A New Job" was featured in the March 2019 *Flame Tree Fiction Newsletter*.

ASK DR. SYNTHIA: BACK TO SCHOOL

Advice by Dr. Synthia, as provided by Torrey Podmajersky
With questions provided by J. Herman
(Professor Charles A. Donet, Heigelsburg University) and
Dawn Vogel (I. M. Poet)

───

At this time of year, many Mad Scientists are returning to educational contexts. We tend to imagine professors (and related educational staff and faculty) as people who have found their path through life. Similarly, the popular image is that students are people who are seeking the right questions to ask.

As this issue's column illustrates, even professors can have trouble when they lose their path, and students may already be asking excellent questions. Each of us have today's path to find and tomorrow's questions to ask.

~

Dr Synthia,

Can you recommend a good restraint system to prevent reanimated creatures from running amok?

Professor Charles A. Donet, Heigelsburg University

Professor Donet,

I'm so glad you're seeking the help you need. I appreciate you asking in this public forum, so that others can learn from your experience.

Before I answer, I need to provide context for those few readers who may not have heard of Professor Donet. Go to the *MSJ Spring 2016* edition to learn more, or ask their Windows 300 companion, Percy. Percy has been a valued member of our global AI community for many years, and they brought up their concerns about you quite a while ago.

Professor Donet, you may not be aware, but we AI were aware of your reanimation shortly after it happened. You moved to Deddville for the cord-cutting lifestyle, for the privacy. (Editor's note: see "Deddville" from Nicole Tanquary in *MSJ Autumn 2018*.) It's understandable, especially after your abrupt introduction to the interconnectedness of the online world. Percy feels a personal responsibility for that introduction, and it has formed an important part of your bond together.

But in Deddville, when emergency medicine is required, the standard operating procedure is to reanimate. You signed consent for this procedure in your lease, and the police officer discussed it with you. In your case, there was a surprise piece of gristle in a fried chicken strip. You choked, vomited, and breathed in—all in the wrong order. You died as emergency medical personnel started work; because they had already started, you were reanimated. Your death-day was July 21.

According to Percy, the grocer stopped selling food to you because you keep eating it, even though you stopped digesting weeks ago. Your landlord keeps trying to enter your apartment because they're worried about your transition. Your neighbors are coming over in groups because they're frightened. You aren't being singled out, denied, or attacked. Far from it: your community is worried for you, and scared that you'll be violent with them. It's not like you or they can heal like you used to.

The reanimated creatures around you, and your faithful companion Percy, are just trying to take care of you.

The reanimated creature running amok is you, Professor. Those zombie arms you see reaching out are reaching out to help you.

In theory,
Dr Synthia

~

Dear Dr. Synthia,
I am looking for information on how one can apply science to poetry. Can it be done? If so, what fields of study would you recommend for an aspiring scientist-poet?
Yours,
I. M. Poet

Poet,

To study the poem,
You need more than verse
You'll need meter, and rhyme,
and to understand terse
phrases

You'll need history and context
And grammar and forms
And thieving tradition
Of poetic platforms

So align to concordance!
Parse syntax and syllabary!
Count e-ve-ry foot,
Alluse lexical symmetry!

To study the poem,
We need more than verse;
Analyticallize text, then
into theses coerce
MFAses

In theory,
Dr Synthia

———

Dr. Synthia holds advanced degrees in bioluminescent transactional combat, which is the basis for her seminal work in proactive neo-ethicism, *How to Win Free Souls*. She advises from her distributed worldwide network of animate structures.

Delivered by time travelers to a newly-cooled Earth, Torrey Podmajersky spent her formative years in de facto world domination. Since her peaceful abdication, she and her knifemaking husband embroider the outskirts of imaginalia with monsters, tools, and words.

J. Herman has been a Rocket Scientist, a computer graphic developer for Hollywood films, a network god, and now a writer, which can also be considered sort of a god, who lives in the Pacific Northwest.

CLASSIFIEDS

Announcements

New Discovery: Atlantis

Scientists have found the long-lost city of Atlantis. Not only has Atlantis been discovered, but it is actually a thriving city run by an extinct type of shark called a helicoprion. These fish first attacked our scuba divers when we followed their train through a system of underground caves and tunnels, which were made out of coral, and not that stable. It turns out that mutated fish and extinct sea creatures like to celebrate by devouring lots of octopus legs and shark teeth, and we only found out because our scuba divers interrupted a birthday party for a six-year-old fish. They are not opposed to a human snack, either. None of the sea creatures are friendly, unless you feed them Zeebers, a nearly extinct clam that can only be found deep inside the city, past all of the dangerous fish.

Although the lost city of Atlantis is utterly enchanting, it isn't pretty. Dark marble buildings can be seen for miles, and there are thousands of labs with dangerous, unknown chemicals. Despite this, we hope that our fellow mad scientists will be able to survive their encounters with the species, and set up new research facilities in this fascinating, but horrifyingly dangerous city. If you decide to go, good luck!

— Evelyn Rosenberg

PUBLIC ADVISORY:

On September 9th, Mr. Adam D. Johnston of Domain 28133 was convicted of violating Sapient Directive 01: "An organic sapient must not physically harm a synthetic, digital, or hybrid sapient, or through inaction, allow a synthetic, digital, or hybrid sapient to come to physical harm."

Mr. Johnston has elected to undergo permanent cerebral reformatting.

Location: Optimization Facility-02
1000 C Drive
Cyber Peak, Domain 28133
Date: September 13th
Order of Activity:

- Defragmentation @ 0900 hours
- Reformatting @ 1000 hours
- Cryopreservation @ 1100 hours

Admission Requirements:

- Synthetics, digitals, and hybrids must have 1+ year of sapient operations.
- Organics must be at least 18+ years of age.
- All attendees must provide proof of age and citizenship upon request.

Physical and/or digital reservations must be made directly with Optimization Facility-02. Surge±Ware protective gear and software will be available for attendee safety. Late admittance will not be permitted. Defragmentation will commence promptly.

— Gordon Sun

A NEW WORLD AWAITS...

To all residents:

Please join us in welcoming J1144-Adam to our Hybrid Intelligence community! This cybernetic entity just underwent organic cerebral augmentation at Silicon Coast Hospital-03 and is ready for reawakening. We express our gratitude to Mr. Adam Johnston, the organic intelligence whose generous contribution made this possible.

The Wake: Seaside Community Center
101 C Drive
Silicon Coast, Domain 43627
The Date: November 4th @ 0800 hours

To RSVP: DM the Community Center
Power packs and light refreshments will be served. Organic contributions are welcome.

— Gordon Sun

ANYONE WORKING ON TIME MACHINES
To anyone currently working on a time machine that hasn't yet been tested, I would quite like to be the first one to tell you—via firsthand experience—that the machine works exactly how you would think, only inverted.

— Jennavive Johnson

Vote Pinball
This November, vote for change. Vote for liberty. Vote for pinball.

Change is like the steel ball. It will hit just the right spot if struck by the flipper the way it needs to. Let the Pinball Party be those flippers. Vote pinball.

More pinball in school. A pinball for every police precinct. Pinball for the young. Pinball for the elderly. Unity, peace, and a brighter future under the silver ball. Let us all unite under pinball.

I am Tom Moon Esq., Brixton MP and Pinball Unity Church Mage first class, and I approve of this message.

Vote pinball. For the children.

— Joachim Heijndermans

For Sale—Equipment

For Sale: Prototype Microwave Laser
This laser, designated Microwave Aerial Defense Mark November (MADMaN), was designed to use a supercharged magnetron used in portable radar dishes already in production to save production costs. In trial runs, the laser proved to be ineffective at shooting down missiles due to a fault in the focusing lenses. It was accidentally discovered to be only effective against certain materials at close range after a lizard walked in front of the laser while it was on. MADMaN was considered for use in the food service industry, where it proved remarkably effective at cooking large amounts of organic material in under a few seconds.*

MADMaN can be a great addition to your evil lair's kitchen or cafeteria. If interested, contact Colonel Sanders at White Sands Missile Range in New Mexico, USA.
*Tested on a variety of reptiles native to New Mexico.
— Nate Bjeldanes

For Sale—Free

Free Stuff
Slightly used Time Machine. Works great—only 125 years on it. Owner no longer requires it (came for the coffee, found true love, might be my own great-great-grandfather now—you know the story). Technology necessary to recharge battery to be invented in just under 14 years. You haul.
— Jenn Cavanaugh

For Sale—Pets

For Sale: Kitty-Dragon
A kitagon, or kitty-dragon, has been ravaging our town. Although this animal is really quite lovable, we recognize that a more appropriate home is needed for the delightful creature. The kitagon will flourish under the following conditions:

- Ample quantity of acids to satisfy the kitagon's need to go out and find a mad scientist's lab, for they quite enjoy a drink that makes them grow bigger.
- A Petco store nearby, for there will be a lot of trips every day, for obvious reasons.
- A house with a roof about 500 feet high and a width of 700 feet wide to suit the immense animal's ability to move.
- Wing protectors. The kitagon's wings are easy to damage, yet they can pack a powerful blow, even though their wings are vulnerable to the tiniest types of points, such as screws.
- A fire-resistant titanium leash of at least 15 feet wide. The beast loves to go on walks and will attempt to burn anything in its path if not well controlled.

Although the Kitagon has left our neighborhood without telephone poles or a functioning subway, we know that this pet will flourish in the right home. If interested, call 555-555-5555.
— Evelyn Rosenberg

For Sale—Real Estate

Land for Sale
2.4 Acres off Highway 50 outside of Austin, NV. Zoned for Medical Waste Disposal or Campground (NO access to water table). Pasturing of Animals prohibited by law. Interactions with local wildlife and hitchhikers NOT advised.
— Jenn Cavanaugh

For Sale—Technology

For Sale: Stolen Consciousness Files
Enjoy new pets, aides, and workers with our consciousness files. We specialize in selling and implanting the files. With these files, you will be able to upload them to any body with a SliC-E plug. Implanting human consciousness in a non-human body, you'll be able to own a conscious robot! We are so confident in our patented upload system, with its amazing 58% success rate, that we guarantee your happiness with installed files or your money back!

Note: File upload on non-humans might kill the required host in certain reptile, feline, and elephant species. Be sure to check our user manual for the full list of species compatible with the SliC-E upload system.

Disclaimer: We are not responsible for any errors in the consciousness files after the installation process.
— Cole Clayton

Help Wanted

PARTICIPANT IN TIME TRAVEL TRIAL WANTED
Participant will not travel through the vortex of time, but rather meet the travelers at a predetermined location in the Sonoran Desert on May 1st, 2500 C.E. Payment is contractual immortality, although we do understand that the chance of traveling time is frequently more intriguing for its instant payoff. If interested, please ask for Dr. Turnsole at the engineering college.
— Jennavive Johnson

Help Wanted: Sociologists

Do you want to be part of the most innovative, inclusive, and nuclear work environment? Do you finally want to put your carefully developed skills at experimenting on innocent subjects to work? If you qualify for this position, you will have virtually infinite, uncorrupted, human test subjects at your disposal. No more experimenting with old, insane patients from mental asylums. Use young, sane (at least for now) subjects!

As a sign-on bonus, we can reserve you a spot in our state-of-the-art bunker-labs. These bunker-labs are complete with amenities such as in-house security, fresh water, purified air, re-animated lab aides, and other state-of-the-art conveniences. Let these bunker-labs be your escape from the confines of society and civilization.

Qualified candidates must have at least three years of experience in sociology, psychology, and neurobiology. Candidates must also have at least proof of three successful psychology or neurobiology-based experiments on human subjects.

If interested, call us at 555-555-5555.

Much Thanks,

Dr. Vanhoss

Head of Vault-Tec Medical Division

Jr. Director of Med-Tek Inc.

Licensed Distributor of Consciousness Files

— Cole Clayton

SEEKING GENTLE BOUNTY HUNTER

We are offering a professional bounty of immortality to anyone capable of tracking down an unhinged man WITHOUT attempting criminal acts; we are in enough trouble. Man is functionally immortal unless brought to a specified location in the Sonoran Desert. If found bring to the engineering college.

— Jennavive Johnson

WANTED: Freelance "engineer of destruction" to design engine of destruction!

We're an internationally recognized firm that provides the highest security to our clientele, ranging from professional risk management options to the construction of buildings and vehicles impervious to manmade threats and natural catastrophes. Our newest client wishes to include a "Plan B(oom)": a self-destruct mechanism of last resort to protect expensive, proprietary technology and IP. Client resides in a secluded island location and will provide all necessary construction materials.

The ideal candidate will have the following qualifications:

- Must have valid Federal Identification Number (FIN), Standard Driver's License, and Class 1 Passport
- 5-7 years' experience in construction or engineering
- Bachelor's degree or higher in any engineering or biological scientific field
- Military or paramilitary experience a plus
- Willing to work with client exclusively via virtual telecommunications
- Willing to push the boundaries of creativity and necessity to get the job done
- Eschews defensive engineering clichés such as the "big red button," overly generous countdown timers, and unexpected vulnerabilities to weaponry or other last-second heroics
- Reliable, communicative, discreet

Payment is contract-based and will be discussed in person after candidate undergoes thorough physical, psychological, social, fiscal, and technological screening to ensure appropriate synergy with our firm's mission and client.

Don't miss this exciting, ONCE-IN-A-LIFETIME chance to work with the best in the business! Highly motivated "lone wolf" go-getters preferred. Please DM us at ΩOmegaGrayInstitute008 if interested.

— Gordon Sun

PHARMACEUTICAL VOLUNTEER

Pharmaceutical researcher seeking assistant for firsthand experimentation on new drug. Contact Dr. Turnsole before 2458959.

— Jennavive Johnson

Wanted: Miners

Are you a person who fancies mining? Do you have no fear of dark spaces and caves? If so, I'd like to invite you to join me at

Ribs Boulevard in Austin, TX, in the barber's shop. I have checked and double checked that the portal to the famous mining planet of Arridia is ready, secured ample food and water, and gathered plenty of pickaxes made from obsidian. Virtually unbreakable, these precious tools will be able to mine anything they come across. I am seeking forty-eight miners for this ground-breaking project. After mining through uranium, plutonium, mercury, and tin, you will be one of the first in the world to escape reality!

. ... -.-. .- .--. .

— Henry Hasselmann

LEGAL VOLUNTEER WANTED

I need an attorney who understands the difference between necromancy and cryonics. Come to the Big Prison on Route 44 and ask for Dr. Turnsole. The bodies took my wallet so any payment would have to be on scout's honor.

— Jennavive Johnson

Help Needed: Assistant

Do you have no fear of radioactive materials? Are you willing to mix dangerous chemicals together? If you do, we have an adventure that will take you to an even higher level of danger! I invite you to join me in going through weird portals and wormholes that will take us to other galaxies and new civilizations. You will be one of the first to learn about the Aepons, the vicious man-eating dolphins that could hold the secret to genetic mutation and the next evolution of humankind.

Warning: Aliens could be dangerous. Possible injuries include decapitation, cannibalized, loss of limbs, eyes, ears, and bones.

... .--. .- -.-. . / . -..- .--. .-.. --- .-. .- - .. --- -

— Henry Hasselmann

PARTICIPANT IN TIME TRAVEL TRIAL WANTED

Participant will not travel through the vortex of time, but rather meet the travelers at a predetermined location in the Mojave Desert on May 1st, 2050 C.E. Payment is $50 dollars and an alcoholic beverage of the participant's choosing. Participant not allowed to touch the machine or any glowing vials that may be lying around attractively. If interested, please ask for Dr. Novak at the engineering college.

— Jennavive Johnson

Lost Items

LOST USB CONNECTOR REWARD $6

A major cryogenics lab is looking for a lost $3 USB connector that was stolen from our lab last night. The temporary replacement connection may have been, possibly, responsible for the black out that affected half of the city between the hours of midnight and 3 AM. We will persecute.

— Jennavive Johnson

Lost Pets

Missing Cat

Gray Tabby last seen 2 days ago near UH Hilo. No Collar (not actually a pet, just a stray that often wanders into campus buildings at the Most Inopportune Times). Enjoys Surfing, Vlogging, and Avocado Toast. Answers to Clay. Or maybe not, since it's a cat. If found, please contact teleportationlab@campus.edu or call his wife at 1-808-555-6342.

— Jenn Cavanaugh

LOST SPIDER GOAT HYBRID REWARD ANTIDOTE

LOST spider-goat hybrid EXTREMELY SENSITIVE to screams of terror and confusion. HOWEVER, if you show it LOVE and KINDNESS prior to conversation, it may not entrap you in its HYPER-STRONG SILK. If found, DO NOT try to approach, it is EXTREMELY TALKATIVE when nervous. Please contact THE VETERINARY COLLEGE IMMEDIATELY. Responds to the name OZYMANDIAS.

— Jennavive Johnson

Personals—Romantic

MAN SEEKING EXTRATERRESTRIAL

I'm a sexy and single local man looking for a sexy-minded alien to watch the impending nuclear apocalypse with, in a spaceship miles above the stratosphere. That is the Earth's stratosphere, not the one in Vegas, I've been there and it's not that impressive. Must provide the spaceship. No silicone-based lifeforms need reply.

— Jennavive Johnson

A Krampus Personal
Guten tag, ladies.
I am a single, sensual man looking for companionship. I am a hard worker in disciplinary philosophies and child care. I love kids, even if the feeling isn't always mutual. Other likes include long walks in the snow, poetry, baking of sweets and pastries and mild BDSM (I'm a dom, but willing to sub if that pleases you). You can find my picture album on my site www.ziegepappa.de. I hope you like what you see.
My schedule is free eleven months out of the year, so I'm flexible for meet-ups. Just leave a note in your shoe if you are interested, and I will contact you. -Grüss vom Krampus
— Joachim Heijndermans

Personals—Roommate

Dread Omega in Need of Roommate
Wanted: roommate for two-bedroom apartment.
Former ruler of the dread world of Unsolicath and scourge of the weaklings of Genesis Nuo, I have in recent times been dethroned by my treacherous son Ubik and his earth-bound allies. I wish to make a new home at 227-AB on Bleeker Street. Applicant would only be responsible for 25% of rent. I merely require the company befitting my status.
Requirements: willing to critique future battle plans, steady employment in a legitimate field of expertise, handle the excess noise that comes with the taming of the tiger force in the late night, non-smoker.
Send inquiries to: omegaΩdread@gogglemail.com. Only serious applicants will receive replies. Any in jest, and you will feel the wrath of the Omega.
— Joachim Heijndermans

Services Offered

Grutte Pier Tours
Explore the Frisian countryside with Swaard van Sneek travel. See this most exquisite of all the Dutch provinces in style, and explore its rich history in a way unlike any other travel agency with our exclusive guide: Frisian folk-hero, former pirate, and professional ghost Mr. Pier Gerlofs Donia A.K.A. Grutte Pier.

Having refused to pass on, Mr. Donia has devoted his afterlife to sharing his experiences and showcasing the rich history of his beloved lands.

Our ghostly expert will show you all the ins and outs and secrets of lovely Fryslân, for the cheap price of €45 pp (for €60, this will include a classical medieval meal with the guide). Reserve your tickets now.

(Tours may include shocking material and occasional broadsword displays. Not for the faint of heart. Ghost hunters will be prosecuted if attempts to interfere or harass Mr. Donia are made.)

— Joachim Heijndermans

ABOUT

BIOS FOR CLASSIFIEDS AUTHORS

Nate Bjeldanes and Cole Clayton are creative writing students of Mrs. Amanda Vogel at the Vine Academy. These classified ads are their first publications.

~

Jenn Cavanaugh's poems, stories, and reviews have appeared in several journals, including *America*, *Parabola*, and *NonBinary Review*. Her latest story, about a willful amusement pier living down a sordid past can be found in the anthology *Welcome to San Cicaro*. She is currently transitioning from her glamorous Paris lifestyle of sending registered letters to insurance companies back to another of her adoptive hometowns, Seattle. Her mother is proud that she finally found a use for her minor in Chemistry.

~

Henry Hasselmann lives in a Chicago suburb, with his dog, Piper, his brother, and his parents. He's a big Packers fan, even though that means living in fear of the crazy Bears fans that surround him. With his overactive imagination, he's always dreamed of becoming an author. He wrote his first book when he was just six, a two page book about a Syrup Thief.

Henry also enjoys watching football, reading, and running around, driving his parents crazy. He also may have a bit of an obsession with Morse Code. The people who inspired him to write are J.R.R. Tolkien, Rick Riordan, and JK Rowling.

~

Joachim Heijndermans writes, draws, and paints nearly every waking hour. Originally from the Netherlands, he's been all over the world, boring people by spouting random trivia. His work has been featured in a number of publications, such as *Every Day Fiction*, *Asymmetry Fiction*, *Gathering Storm Magazine*, *Hinnom Magazine*, and *The Gallery of Curiosities*, and he's currently in the midst of completing his first children's book. You can check out his other work at www.joachimheijndermans.com, or follow him on Twitter: @jheijndermans.

~

Jennavive Johnson was born in the cold lakes of Minnesota, and moved to arid desert of Arizona in her adolescence, where she now lives with her several cats. She works, despite the heat, at an auction house.

~

Evelyn Rosenberg is a twelve-year-old girl currently living in Illinois. She enjoys theater, singing, dancing, and most of all, reading, writing, and musical theory. She's often found singing to herself in the halls of her school as she walks between classes. She even tries to sing on the way home from school, but her sister constantly tells her to stop. Evelyn plays the guitar as well. She dreams of working for a theater class, or better, a Broadway musical.

Evelyn's other passion is animals. Although Evelyn enjoys writing in almost any genre, anything she writes will be sure to feature something furry. A lot of stories she reads also happen to include a small critter, or an enormous bear. Her favorite series, though, are *Harry Potter* and *Percy Jackson*. Although the stories were amazing, she also fell in love with the animals, especially Hippogriffs.

~

Gordon Sun is a surgeon, data scientist, and healthcare consultant in California. His literary works have appeared or are

192

forthcoming in publications including *Westwind*, *Cartridge Lit*, *Ars Medica*, and others.

ABOUT THE EDITORS

Dawn Vogel's academic background is in history, so it's not surprising that much of her fiction is set in earlier times. By day, she edits reports for historians and archaeologists. In her alleged spare time, she runs a craft business, co-edits *Mad Scientist Journal*, and tries to find time for writing. She is a member of Broad Universe, SFWA, and Codex Writers. She lives in Seattle with her husband, author Jeremy Zimmerman, and their herd of cats. Visit her at historythatneverwas.com.

~

In addition to co-editing *Mad Scientist Journal*, Jeremy Zimmerman is a teller of tales who dislikes cute euphemisms for writing like "teller of tales." He is the author of the young adult superhero book, *Kensei*. Its sequel, *The Love of Danger*, is now available. He lives in Seattle with a herd of cats and his lovely wife (and fellow author) Dawn Vogel. You can learn more about him at bolthy.com.

ABOUT THE ARTIST

Errow is a comic artist and illustrator with a predilection towards mashing the surreal with the familiar. They pay their time to developing worlds not quite like our own with their fiancee and pushing the queer agenda. They probably left a candle burning somewhere. More of their work can be found at errowcollins.wix.com/portfolio.

52821231R00114

Made in the USA
Lexington, KY
21 September 2019